W9-BTF-508

FRANKLIN ELEMENTARY
33007070030669

STARFISH

FRANKLIN SCHOOL
MEDIA CENTER

STARFISH

A NOVEL

JAMES CROWLEY

ILLUSTRATIONS BY

JIM MADSEN

Disney • HYPERION BOOKS
New York

Text copyright © 2010 by James Crowley
Illustrations copyright © 2010 by Jim Madsen

All rights reserved. Published by Disney • Hyperion Books, an imprint of Disney Book Group. No part of this book may be reproduced or transmitted in any form or by any means, electronic or mechanical, including photocopying, recording, or by any information storage and retrieval system, without written permission from the publisher. For information address Disney • Hyperion Books, 114 Fifth Avenue, New York, New York 10011-5690.

First Edition
1 3 5 7 9 10 8 6 4 2
V567-9638-5-10121
Printed in the United States of America

This book is set in 13.5 point Fournier MT.
Designed by Elizabeth H. Clark

Library of Congress Cataloging-in-Publication Data on file.

ISBN 978-1-4231-2588-4

Reinforced binding

Visit www.hyperionbooksforchildren.com

THIS LABEL APPLIES TO TEXT STOCK

For Doc and Jude

BARNEY'S CAMP
Great Wood
COLLAPSED LODGE
GARDEN
Cliff
Winding Creek
CANADA
MONTANA
area of detail
Milk River
BLACKFEET RESERVATION
Heart Butte
Birch Creek

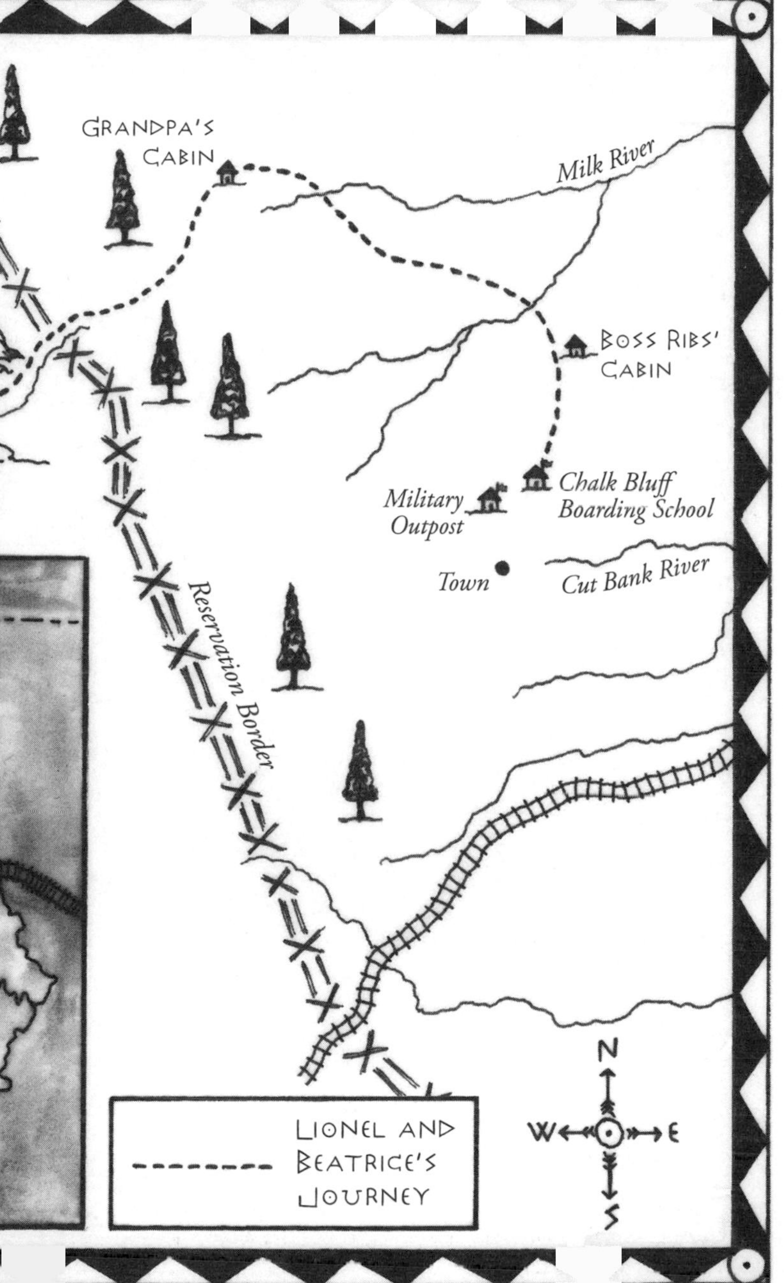

GRANDPA'S CABIN
Milk River
BOSS RIBS' CABIN
Chalk Bluff Boarding School
Military Outpost
Town
Cut Bank River
Reservation Border
N
W
E
S
LIONEL AND BEATRICE'S JOURNEY

Prologue

The snow that fell through the night let up near morning but continued to swirl and whip around the government barracks and outbuildings of the Chalk Bluff Indian reservation. Against a night sky, the structures' silhouettes looked like ghostly ships crossing the desolate, rolling hills of the high Montana plain.

An old man felt his way along the buildings, his gnarled hand brushing against the neglected, paint-peeled walls. In his other hand, he clutched a bottle and the corner of a tattered gray army blanket, which he fought to keep wrapped around his shoulders.

The old man steadied himself, drew a long pull

of corn liquor from the heavy green glass bottle, then stumbled toward the small corral that ran adjacent to the barracks. He remembered the days before there were buildings like this, or of any kind, on the land—the days when he had been known as a great warrior, a great hunter. But that was a long time ago. Now he was known as a drunk.

The old man reached the corral and fell to his knees in a deep bank of snow. He mumbled a song, and the singing seemed to summon a shadowy presence from the darkness. The man looked up at the shadow, the snow landing in tiny wet kisses on his face.

As the shadow moved closer, the old man let the army blanket drop from his shoulders. A string of heavy bear claws hung from his withered neck. He pulled the strand over his head, reached out to the night, and collapsed.

STARFISH

PART ONE

CHAPTER ONE

BEATRICE & THE POTBELLIED STOVE • THE BOARDING SCHOOL • THEIR HISTORY

LIONEL WOKE to a familiar drip. An icicle had appeared in the corner of the window next to his bed one night and had proceeded, over the course of the winter, to find a way through the seam of the frame and into the barrack. In the fading moonlight, he watched as a single droplet of water wound slowly down the icicle's smooth contours. From there, Lionel knew, it would pass over the frozen and rotting wood of the windowsill, then hold for a moment before dropping with annoying regularity into the small puddle beside his bed.

The steady plinking sound reminded Lionel of the piano that the Brothers who ran the Chalk Bluff boarding school played from time to time. As Lionel lay listening to the monotonous drops, he heard another sound—the faint hint of movement coming from the girls' end of the barrack.

The girls and boys had once lived in separate barracks, but ever since the girls' bunkhouse had burned to the ground, they had been housed in opposite ends of the same building. Lionel stared down the long dark hall toward his older sister, Beatrice. He watched as she threw back her heavy covers, pushed the hair from her face, and crept to the pot-bellied stove that separated the girls' and boys' sides

of the bunkhouse. Beatrice was three years older than Lionel, but he and everyone else on the Blackfeet Indian reservation knew that she was already beyond her twelve years. Lionel had heard older people say that it was because Beatrice stood watch at their mother's bedside while she died of tuberculosis in the winter of 1903. Others said that Beatrice was just born old, as some people are.

There had never been any photographs of their mother, so Lionel had no way of knowing if the image he carried of her in his head was in any way accurate. When he questioned his sister, she described their mother as having long black hair and strong arms, so that is how Lionel saw her.

"But, it don't matter no more," Beatrice would say about their mother's passing. "She died a long time before that hospital bed. She died years ago, the day they started calling our land this here reservation."

After their mother's death, Beatrice and Lionel had been sent to the boarding school, where they had lived for the last six years. The school was run by the Brothers from the church, and while not directly overseen by the government, the proximity of the soldiers' outpost inevitably led to their involvement in maintaining the peace and some semblance of order. Beatrice complained to Lionel that they were not allowed to leave the reservation without the superintendent's permission. Lionel often wondered where they would go if they had been allowed, and why this bothered Beatrice so, but it did.

Beatrice's flannel pajamas were visible as they hung from beneath the layers of sweaters and the heavy wool pants she now wore. The pajamas had been a gift from the army captain of the nearby post, when it was learned that Beatrice and Lionel's father had also died. No one seemed to know how or why their father died, but Beatrice was given the pajamas and Lionel was given a small army sack jacket identical to the one that the captain wore from time to time. The captain, who Lionel thought was a nice man, had tried to give Beatrice a jacket, but Beatrice refused to wear it no matter how cold it was, so she ended up with the pajamas.

Lionel liked the captain and the ribbon medals he sometimes wore on his jacket. He knew the captain because brushing down the captain's big bay stallion was one of Lionel's morning chores. The horse was the small military outpost's pride and joy. The captain called him Ulysses, and he was thought to be the fastest horse in Montana. Beatrice said that an association of horse enthusiasts came all the way from Billings by train one time just to watch him run.

From his bed, Lionel watched his sister adjust the damper, stir the embers, then add another piece of dusty black coal. He was always amazed that Beatrice was able to move without making a sound. He lost her for a moment in the darkness but heard the distant punctuated sigh of her bunk as she slipped back beneath the heavy woolen blankets to wait for morning.

Lionel lay listening to the breathing of the other children who slept around them under their piles of army-issued blankets. He waited for his sister's breath to fall into the same easy cadence, but it did not come.

"O'káát!" Beatrice suddenly spoke, telling Lionel to sleep, in the native tongue of their people. And although she spoke softly, it wasn't a whisper.

"You're going to get whipped if they hear you're not speaking in the English," Lionel warned.

"Nítssksinii'pa," Beatrice replied.

"They'll whip ya real good if they hear you been out of bed."

Beatrice did not answer, and again Lionel heard the slow drip of the icicle. It seemed far away now, but soon transformed into the very present ringing of Brother Finn's brass bell.

CHAPTER TWO

BEATRICE IS WARNED • ULYSSES •
THE FROZEN MAN • BEAR CLAWS •
SERGEANT HASKELL JENKINS &
PRIVATE SAMUEL LUMPKIN

LIONEL SAT up with a start. Brother Finn had shoved his bunk and was shouting in Latin, "Up. Up. Today is your day to serve the Lord our Savior!"

Lionel's eyes followed Brother Finn's long black robes as they swept down the narrow rows of the barrack. The other children got up from their bunks, pulling off their nightclothes and dressing for the day—everyone but Beatrice. Brother Finn stopped at the foot of her bunk and stared into the jumbled mess of bedding.

"Let's go, Beatrice. Let's not start the Lord's day this way," Brother Finn announced in English.

Beatrice appeared from beneath her blankets and pushed the hair from her face.

"And today is the day that your hair will be cut. You've been warned. You will report to the barber after Mass. Now, let's go!"

Brother Finn continued down the row and out the other end of the room, but his cries still echoed through the barrack. Beatrice crawled out of bed and pulled on her patchwork school uniform.

Beatrice's uniform was different from those of the other thirty-three children who attended the school. To start, it wasn't as new; the rich navy blue color had faded, and it seemed to be more patch than original material. The Brothers told Beatrice repeatedly that she should report to the quartermaster for a new issue, but she preferred what she now wore.

Lionel looked at his sister. Her hair was dramatically longer than the rest of the children's. It was thick—he supposed like their mother's—and so dark that it shone almost blue in the morning light. Lionel's hair was cropped close to his scalp, as short as the outpost's barber's shears could cut.

"*You'll be whipped if they hear you're out of bed,*"

Beatrice called down the row, imitating her brother's voice. She smiled at Lionel and turned to make her bunk.

Lionel pulled his blanket tight at the corners. He couldn't believe his sister's stupidity.

"You will," Lionel warned again, "and you know it."

Lionel stepped from the relative warmth of the bunkhouse into the weak light of a late winter's sun. He walked in silence except for the crunch of old snow that lay a few inches under the fresh. Around him, the neighboring outpost came to life. He heard, but no longer listened to, the different calls of the army men's bugle, the rustling and rousing of livestock, and the drone and drill of military life to which he had become accustomed. Lionel watched Beatrice and some of her classmates as they poured from the girls' side of the barrack on their way to Mass.

Beatrice's hair was tied into two thick braids. She had been allowed to keep her long hair as she had been in the infirmary when the new regulations came from the East. The latest rules defined the manner in which the girls' hair should be cut, and stated that they would now have a new and different uniform.

Lionel watched as Beatrice wandered in her tattered clothes behind the rest of the girls and in particular Delores Ground. Delores and the other girls proudly wore the new issue, oddly cut dresses that Lionel thought resembled the uniforms of the army men that worked on the water. The captain called them "sailors" and had shown Lionel a picture of the men standing on the bow of a great ship. The men wore white uniforms with wide collars, like Delores's.

Lionel had a hard time trying to imagine Beatrice with the short bobbed hair and in a dress like the ones the rest of the girls now wore. But he knew that he would soon see it for himself, as the Brothers and the captain were not likely to let her slide on regulations now that she was no longer sick.

Beatrice joined Lionel, and together they walked toward the corrals, where Lionel slipped between the snow-covered pine poles. He glanced at Beatrice and thought of their grandfather, who did not want to live near the actual agency and had chosen instead his own "reservation," a small plot on the banks of the Milk River near the northern end of the Blackfeet's allotted lands. It was, Beatrice said, a good day's ride from the school.

Lionel watched as his sister turned away from the corral and stood with her back to the rising sun. She angled herself slightly to the north, to their grandfather and the great mountains that broke through the low snow clouds.

She dug into her pocket and pulled out a small tobacco pouch made from the soft underbelly of a buffalo calf that their grandfather had found frozen one late-spring morning. He had given Beatrice the pouch on her ninth birthday, and she still practiced what he had taught her, despite the Brothers' and soldiers' rules.

Beatrice opened the smooth leather pouch and removed a small plug of tobacco. She worked the dark leaves in her hands and then raised them, holding the tobacco out in front of her. She held it above her head, offering it to a jagged mountain peak that was the easternmost tip of what the army referred to as the Rocky Mountains.

The army and Brothers from the school called the broken section of the mountain "Chief Mountain." They said that movement from within the earth had caused its eastern wall to separate, and now it lay in jumbled piles of rubble among the small foothills.

Their grandmother had once told them that the mountain fell because the Blackfeet no longer had their sacred Beaver Woman as a spiritual leader. She said that because of this, they had lost their way and had been forced to settle down as opposed to continuing their nomadic life following the great herds of buffalo across the northern plains. She said that this forced the buffalo to leave, although they were waiting for the Blackfeet somewhere. Lionel often wondered where.

Beatrice let some of the tobacco slip through her fingers and then watched as it floated off toward the north. She turned west, holding the tobacco as an offering, then south, her eyes passing over Cut Bank Ridge and eventually stopping as she faced Heart Butte. She held the tobacco out toward Heart Butte, then turned east to the endless expanse of snow-covered grass before her. Lionel could see Beatrice's lips move as she sang a song quietly to herself. He felt a slight breeze from the north as if somebody or something were actually listening.

He lowered his head and thought of the day that

they were told their grandmother had also gone on to join their parents. Then Lionel turned with the wind, crossed the corral, and climbed out the other side. He stood above the water trough, looking down at the thick layer of ice that had formed overnight. He scuffed his feet through the snow at the trough's base, searching for the rock that he stored there for the specific chore of breaking the ice.

As he shuffled along, Lionel looked over his shoulder. The schoolhouse and chapel loomed some fifty paces away on the hill above him. He hoped that no one was watching what Beatrice was up to, as it would surely end with her getting in trouble. Lionel did not understand Beatrice's fascination with the older traditions, and he definitely did not understand how they could possibly be worth the troubles they caused. He turned to warn her again, but was interrupted on his way by a soft nuzzle from Ulysses.

"Good morning, Ulysses," he said softly to the horse, not taking his eyes off his sister. "Look at her, will you? Sometimes I think Beatrice tries to get us in trouble."

Lionel wrapped his arms around the horse's thick neck and entangled his hands in his long mane for warmth. Ulysses, who normally would stand still for hours with this kind of attention, rocked his head and shifted his weight from hoof to hoof.

"What is it, boy? You hungry? Thirsty?" Lionel asked. He thought it must be the feed. Ulysses often grew hungrier over the long snowy nights.

"Okay, okay, I've got to find my rock." Lionel dug through the snow. "I'll get you started with some water."

Ulysses continued to shift uncomfortably, making short guttural noises that Lionel thought resembled a hog more than a Great War Horse.

"What's with you this morning?" Lionel followed the horse's gaze and discovered the source of his discomfort. There was a man kneeling, almost in a pile, at the far end of the corral. Ulysses trotted the length of the corral, and stopped, as if waiting for Lionel to follow.

"Hello?" Lionel heard the word escape from his mouth, more in the form of a question than a greeting. The man did not move.

Lionel slowly made his way toward the silent figure. "Are you all right?"

Lionel knew the answer to his question before

he had even asked it. The kneeling man was frozen. Frozen solid. His exposed skin was the fading gray color of the morning, and a silver layer of frost covered him from head to toe. In one hand, almost as though he were handing it to Lionel, was a string of bear claws; in the other hand was a green glass bottle.

Lionel looked around, unsure of what to do. He knew that he should run immediately, right now, and find the captain or Brother Finn, but he didn't move. Lionel was frozen. Frozen like the man. Frozen to the man.

"Mister?" Lionel's voice cracked as he pulled off his mittens. He reached his arm toward the man's outstretched hand, toward the string of bear claws.

The claws felt smooth beneath Lionel's fingers, and the warmth of his skin immediately melted the frost that covered the shiny black of each claw and the intricate beading on the woven leather straps that held them together. Something within Lionel told him to take them. They seemed to be offered. He actually didn't see it as taking so much as liberating the claws from the cold, frozen hand.

Lionel pulled at the string, but was surprised to

find that the small tugs did little to release the necklace. Something within spoke again, telling him to pull harder, so he did. He yanked at it with a short, quick motion, freeing the bear claws but not without a price. Lionel felt the necklace break, and stumbled backward, holding what had once been a circle, but was now a long string of bear claws.

"Say, there." A voice from behind startled Lionel. "Say, boy, what the hell ya doin' over there?"

Lionel spun around, slipping the claws into his coat pocket. There stood Sergeant Haskell Jenkins.

"Who you got with ya in the snow there?" Jenkins spat. His words had a slight slur to them.

"I-I-I don't know," Lionel stammered, stepping back from the Frozen Man. He hoped that Jenkins hadn't seen him slip the claws into his pocket.

Jenkins moved closer, until he stood above Lionel and the frozen corpse. Lionel looked up into Sergeant Jenkins's face. A jagged scar started at his pointy chin, snaked up and over the left side of his mouth, then continued until it disappeared beneath a coarse black leather patch that covered his left eye. The mark pushed the good side of Jenkins's mouth into what looked to be a permanent sneer, and the patch was crossed with a hobnailed *X*. Jenkins liked to tell people, especially the ladies at Gorence Trading Post, that he had received his alteration at the hands of "fierce savages" in the "defense of this Great Nation." In reality, nothing could be further from the truth. The scar that took one eye and slurred Jenkins's speech was actually the result of a drunken debacle with a log-cutting machine at the Wyoming State Fair. The machine ran a long chainlike blade off of a steam driven engine, and the moment that Jenkins, who offered to demonstrate the contraption, laid the blade on the log, the chain kicked back, buckled, and broke, taking a good chunk of Jenkins's face with it.

Jenkins pulled his wool cap from his head and kicked at the Frozen Man with his shiny black boot.

"Aw, hell boy. Don't be scared. It's just a dead, drunk Indian."

Lionel watched as Jenkins reached down and rifled a few coins from the man's pockets, then pried a hunting knife from the Frozen Man's belt. Jenkins turned and raised a crooked finger to his snarled lips.

"That's our little secret, you understand?" Jenkins said this while drawing the sheathed blade of the Frozen Man's hunting knife across his neck. "Understand?"

Lionel nodded his head as Jenkins pocketed the coins. He was suddenly overcome with a feeling of shame for having taken the Frozen Man's necklace. He thought about what Beatrice had told him about where his father and mother had gone, versus where Brother Finn said they had gone when they died. He wondered where the Frozen Man was off to, and if he might have needed his bear claws with him when he got there.

"I'm guessing that the old chief had a little too much firewater," a familiar voice said.

Lionel looked up into the bad teeth and scraggly beard of Jenkins's running buddy, Private Samuel Lumpkin. "That about right, boy?" Lumpkin continued.

Under different circumstances Lumpkin and Jenkins might not have been friends, but years in the service on the plains had brought them together, and their general disrespect for everything, including themselves, had solidified the deal. Lumpkin knelt down and wrested the bottle from the Frozen Man's hand.

"Spoils of war," Lumpkin said. But as he stood, he startled. On the fence directly in front of him sat Beatrice.

Beatrice looked Lumpkin in the eye with an unnerving intensity. Lumpkin took a step back, still holding the bottle.

"Who in the hell are you?" he asked, collecting himself.

"Beatrice," she answered, her voice steady.

Jenkins took a step toward Beatrice, the Frozen Man still in prayer at his feet.

"Beatrice, huh?" Jenkins slurred. "Well, Beatrice, as I was tellin' yer young schoolmate here, this is our li'l secret."

Ulysses continued to nervously shift and move about the corral behind Beatrice. A bugle blew in the background, which was soon followed by the ringing of Brother Finn's bell. Lionel watched as the children made their way into the chapel, but he knew that his sister would remain where she was, sitting on the rail. She would wait to make sure that the two soldiers didn't do anything more to disrespect the corpse.

"You heard the bell, git!" Jenkins shouted.

Beatrice didn't move, so Lionel didn't move.

Jenkins took another step closer to Beatrice, his hand on the beaded sheath of the knife that he had stolen from the Frozen Man.

"What's a matter with this one? Don't she speak English?" Jenkins asked, turning to Lumpkin, then back to Beatrice. "You deaf? Hard of hearing?"

Jenkins reached out, grabbing a firm hold of Beatrice's patchwork jacket. Beatrice still didn't move, but Ulysses did. The big horse reared back on his hind legs, then rushed the fence, almost ramming it with his head. Private Lumpkin jumped back, knocking Lionel to the ground.

Beatrice remained calmly perched on the fence as though she alone were in control of Ulysses, her own personal cyclone. Sergeant Jenkins hadn't moved either, which seemed to inspire Ulysses to rear back on his hind legs again and paw viciously at the air. The commotion had drawn the attention of Brother Finn, who now stood at the open door.

"What is this?" Brother Finn inquired. "Sergeant, what's going on here?"

"Just another Injun, Monsignor," Lumpkin answered. "But this one's real drunk."

"Private, I've told you before I am not the

Monsignor. Brother Finn will do." He hurried to the Frozen Man and knelt down to feel his forehead.

Jenkins's and Beatrice's eyes were locked. Up on the hill, Lionel saw the captain appear on the porch of his residence.

"Drunk? My Lord and Savior, Private, this man is dead." Flustered, Brother Finn released the Frozen Man. "Alright, you two. Let's go. Time for Mass. We'll have to say a prayer for this poor soul."

Beatrice jumped down from the fence, still eye-ing Lumpkin and Jenkins. More soldiers gathered as Brother Finn urged Lionel and Beatrice toward the chapel. The captain turned back to his quarters, and a soldier entered the corral and tried to calm Ulysses, who still paced, snorting and kicking at the air.

"Don't worry, Brother Finn. We'll see that the man gets a proper Christian burial," Jenkins said. "Whether the heathen deserves it or not."

Brother Finn nodded and continued toward the steps.

"Oh, and Be-a-trice," Jenkins went on, "why don't you come see me after Mass. You're wearin' your hair a tad bit longer than current regulations."

Lionel saw Jenkins give Beatrice a scalping sign

behind Brother Finn's back. Beatrice eyed Jenkins all the way to and up the stairs of the chapel.

"Who in the hell does that creepy little Injun think she is?" Lionel heard Lumpkin shout. He didn't catch what the private said next as the chapel door closed, holding Lionel and Beatrice to the darkness within.

Chapter Three

The Chapel • Gridiron • Beatrice Stands • An Eagle & Three Hawks • Expulsion

The children were restless through Mass, craning their necks to look out the thick stained-glass windows, trying to get a glimpse of the Frozen Man. From where he sat, Lionel could see the soldiers. They passed the Frozen Man's bottle of corn liquor between them, each taking a swig. Lumpkin sat in the snow with his arm around the Frozen Man and held the bottle up before drinking. Then, the men tried, as best they could, to lift the man. But the Frozen Man remained kneeling, his arm outstretched, and this made it difficult.

The priest joined Brother Finn at the altar. They droned on in Latin while Lionel and the rest of the children listened, not really having a clue what they said.

Lionel glanced at Beatrice, who stared silently at the crucifix that hung above the altar. Beatrice once told Lionel that she admired Christ and said that he must have been a great man to be able to face death with such conviction. Lionel saw that Delores Ground was also looking at Beatrice and then at him. He quickly dropped his head and stared down at his shoes.

Lionel and Delores had been partners once when the captain's wife had gathered the children and tried to teach them a dance from the East that she called the Virginia Reel. Lionel thought that he would someday take Delores as his wife, but that was before Barney Little Plume, from the school down by Heart Butte, gave Delores some rock candy in exchange for a kiss.

The children from Heart Butte had come up for a day of athletic competition, and that afternoon, Chalk Bluff played Heart Butte in a game of gridiron football. Beatrice, despite being two years too young to play and a girl, ran with the ball to score on four different occasions. She also, on one of her many tackles, forced Barney to leave the game by breaking his leg. No one could stop Beatrice on that day. Chalk Bluff beat Heart Butte 32–0. After the game, the older men on the tribal council said that if Beatrice had been born a boy, she would have been a great warrior and horseman like her father and grandfather.

The Brothers and soldiers of Chalk Bluff were also impressed with Beatrice's athleticism. They'd even gone so far as to hide from the Brothers who ran the Heart Butte School that Beatrice was a girl. They listed her as "Bill" on the team roster and tied her braids up, hiding them under a leather helmet. They knew that Chalk Bluff could always count on Beatrice. And they were right. In every competition, no matter what it was or who it was against, Beatrice won. That, and the fact that she got so sick, is why Lionel thought Beatrice received different treatment from the Brothers and soldiers than the rest of the students did.

The day of the Heart Butte football game was the last time that Lionel had held Delores Ground's hand. Lionel eyed Delores across the chapel and once again thought that they would not be married after all.

"Now, if everyone will please bow your heads."

Brother Finn broke from his Latin for a moment as the priest prepared the Eucharist for Communion. "Yes, bow your heads and say a prayer for the poor soul whose unfortunate demise was discovered this morning before Mass."

The children did as they were told, some of them pulling out their rosaries and murmuring their way down the many beads. Lionel stole a glance at Beatrice who had begun her prayer, which also started as a low murmur but slowly grew to a chant, then a song. She held her head low, but would occasionally raise her eyes toward the paint-peeled ceiling, her song becoming more and more audible as she went. The priest had asked the children to pray, and as far as Lionel was concerned, he couldn't tell the difference between Brother Finn's prayers in Latin and what Beatrice was singing. He didn't fully understand either of them, so he joined Beatrice.

Lionel's song also started low, but soon grew. As he imitated Beatrice, he began to think about the great green pasture that stood before their grandfather's house and the mountain that towered in the distance above his tiny cabin. He also thought of an eagle and the three hawks that he and Beatrice had seen circling overhead one day. They had watched them until they were only black dots in the bluest of blue skies.

Lionel heard a bell ring and no longer saw the sky. He looked toward the altar where Brother Finn stood glaring at him and Beatrice.

As their singing grew louder, Brother Finn urged them with his eyes to stop, then glanced with apprehension toward the priest, who looked around like an eagle, trying to determine where the song originated. A moment later, the priest was down from the altar and looming above Lionel.

Beatrice continued to sing. So Lionel continued to sing.

"And that will be enough of that there, Miss Beatrice, Mr. Lionel," the priest announced. But the song continued.

Lionel looked out the window at Ulysses pacing restlessly in his corral and then stared down at the cracked, worn leather of his shoes. He continued to sing with Beatrice as Brother Finn tried to continue in Latin. The priest shot a glare at Brother Finn, who grew immediately silent.

"Miss Beatrice, Mr. Lionel, I said that is enough!"

The song stopped.

"I'm trying to pray," Beatrice said firmly.

"Trying to pray by mumbling gibberish to the wind? I most certainly think not." And this the priest punctuated by grabbing Beatrice and Lionel by their ears and yanking them to their feet, as if pulling a pair of jackrabbits from a hole.

And then Beatrice said it.

"What's the difference from whatever the hell you've been mumblin'?"

A collective gasp came from the Brothers and children. Lionel thought that the priest's face would explode. It turned red, then almost purple. The priest jerked them sideways toward the back of the chapel.

"I will not have you disrespecting the Lord with some half-cocked pagan philosophies in His house—or anywhere else, for that matter."

The rest of the children were now on their feet trying to get a clear view. Another Brother, Brother Thomas, stood to make his way toward the priest, who was struggling to get Lionel and Beatrice down the aisle. Brother Thomas reached out as they passed, but missed, tripping over one of the other children and spilling into the aisle with a thud. The entire church erupted with laughter.

Brother Thomas scrambled back to his feet. "Eyes to the front!" he instructed the congregation in a tightened whisper.

"You are in the House of the Lord," the priest continued. "You and your brother, Lionel, will act accordingly or prepare yourself to face the consequence of your actions." The priest shoved them toward the door, but Beatrice suddenly stopped.

"You'll leave my brother alone," she said, as more a matter of fact than anything else.

The priest pulled Beatrice closer. "Is that right, young Beatrice? You're quite bold today, aren't ya? Well, let me tell you something, my young friend, I will not have you disrupting these Holiest of the blessed sacraments."

"Well, they ain't mine," Beatricc replied.

With this, the priest slapped Beatrice across the face. "And I will not have you comparing your heathen rituals to the direct word of our Savior."

The priest pushed Beatrice out the double doors. Lionel tried to follow, but was grabbed by Brother Thomas. Jenkins, Lumpkin, and the other men scrambled to attention, hiding the green glass bottle in the snow.

The priest stood on the top step of the church, his heavy black robes engulfing Beatrice like the wings of a raven. "Sergeant, see to it that Miss Beatrice finds her way to the barber," he said, releasing Beatrice's ear and practically throwing her down the stairs, "and then to the quartermaster. I do not want to see her out of uniform again!"

The priest turned his back on Beatrice. He stepped inside the chapel, shut the doors behind him, then glared at Lionel and the other children as he stormed up the aisle to the altar.

Brother Thomas pulled Lionel down into the pew beside him. "If you're smart, you won't follow your sister's arrogant ways!" he snapped.

Through the stained glass of the windows, Lionel saw the soldiers moving toward Beatrice.

Chapter Four

Sheep Shears • Lionel's Run • Escape • Rolling Seas of Snow

Lionel could hear Ulysses over the soldiers' raised voices and Beatrice's struggle. He could see the great horse running from one side of the corral to the other, kicking out his back legs and snorting at the wind. He craned his neck further and through the dirty colored glass could see the soldiers surround his sister.

"Aye, the Monsignor's patience has run out, has it?" Jenkins shouted. He took hold of the back of Beatrice's shirt and dragged her across the snow toward the water trough and the Frozen Man. "Private Lumpkin, I think we'll save the barber some trouble. Bring them sheep shears from the shed."

Private Lumpkin looked up from the hidden bottle to Sergeant Jenkins.

"Come on." Jenkins's voice grew more impatient. "I ain't have all day to be dedicatin' to the beautification of Injuns."

A small trickle of blood dripped from Beatrice's ear and onto the fresh fallen snow. Lionel saw Beatrice look up at Jenkins and then toward the chapel, but the doors to the chapel were closed.

Lionel watched Lumpkin disappear into the tack room and return with a long pair of rusted iron sheep shears.

"We best be making sure she's clean, first." Jenkins laughed as he yanked Beatrice up and over the side of the trough.

"Eyes in front, now!" Brother Thomas warned, and Lionel turned to the altar and the crucifix. He stared at the silent statue's thorny crown and the blood that ran down the sides of its face. He looked back to Beatrice and watched in horror as Jenkins cracked the ice on top of the trough's cold water with his sister's head.

Lionel looked again to Ulysses and then, without thinking, broke free from Brother Thomas's grip and ran. Brother Thomas tried to follow but tripped, this time over the kneeler. The rest of the children spun around, their eyes following Lionel as he burst out the doors and down the steps.

"Settle down there, let me get ahold of ya," Jenkins continued, forcing Beatrice's head below the water's surface. Beatrice struggled, then seemed to relax, her body still moving but with less fight. "Ah, there we go. Perhaps a bit of a breather."

Jenkins pulled Beatrice's head from the water and stared at her as one might watch a landed fish gasping for its last breath.

"Gimme them shears!" Jenkins barked, his breath smelling of the corn liquor from the Frozen Man's bottle. He shoved Beatrice's head under a second time. Beatrice struggled but again could not break free.

"God damn it, hold still!" Jenkins cried as he tried to get a good grip on Beatrice with one hand, holding the shears with the other. Beatrice briefly broke the surface.

Lionel reached the men and hurled himself at them as best he could by pouncing on Private Lumpkin's back. Lumpkin quickly threw him off, and he landed with a thud against Ulysses's corral.

"What's with you, boy? Have you lost yer mind?"

Lumpkin glanced at Lionel in disbelief before turning back to Beatrice.

Brother Finn and some of the other children appeared on the steps of the chapel. Anger flashed across Brother Finn's face, followed quickly by confusion. Lionel turned to Ulysses, who now stood over him pawing at the muddy dirt, then slipped quietly into the corral.

"Put her back under, that'll get her to stop all that kickin'!" Lumpkin yelled, grabbing ahold of Beatrice and shoving her beneath the surface once again.

"Sergeant!" Brother Finn barked as he ran down the steps toward the trough.

Jenkins set the shears down to readjust his grip on the back of Beatrice's neck. "Alright, let her up."

They pulled Beatrice, gasping, to the surface, and from there everything seemed to happen at once. Beatrice filled her lungs with the cold morning air. She saw the shears on the top of the trough, swept them up, and brought them down hard, pinning Jenkins's hand to the frozen wood. Then, everything stopped.

Jenkins looked at Beatrice, then down. The shears were now perpendicular to the trough, and to Jenkins's hand. A steady stream of blood poured from the wound as if the dark liquid were actually spouting from the shears.

Lumpkin and the other men pulled Beatrice from the top of the trough and dropped her into the bloody snow at its base. Jenkins fell back and tried to free his hand. The pain caught up with him. He turned to Beatrice and growled through clenched teeth, "I'll kill you for this! I swear to God I will kill you!"

The commotion emptied the chapel, adding to the confusion. Children ran screaming. Some stood in shock.

"What is this?" Brother Thomas yelled, as bewildered as the children. "What is this?"

Jenkins pulled the shears from his hand and tried to kick at Beatrice, who scrambled backward out of his reach. Lumpkin and the other soldiers struggled to grab her, but then, in the midst of the uncertainty, there was suddenly a horse. The men fell back as the horse barreled through them toward Beatrice.

Lionel's hands were wound through Ulysses's mane. He rode without regret at the men, and they scattered. Lionel moved toward Beatrice, who lay in the snow trying to catch her breath. As he approached,

Beatrice jumped, and in a single fluid motion, threw her arm around Ulysses's neck and swung up behind her brother onto the horse's back.

The addition of Beatrice seemed to propel Ulysses forward, and soon the three of them were nearing the edge of the tiny outpost. Lionel looked back at the chaos that churned around the trough. He saw the priest, Brother Finn, Brother Thomas, and the soldiers. He saw Delores and the other children. He saw the Frozen Man.

Lionel turned back to the never-ending sea of snow that stretched before them. He buried his head in Ulysses's mane and held on as best he could.

Chapter Five

The Cottonwoods • Snow • The Long Night • Morning • A Small Farm

Beatrice and Lionel rode hard through the day and into the night. They barely spoke, choosing instead to ride in silence, the events of the morning running feverishly through their heads. The snow started back up around dark, and they stopped at a small stream under a cluster of cottonwood trees.

"I guess we best lay up here" was all Beatrice said. She slipped down from Ulysses's back at the water's edge and started to gather the fallen pieces of cottonwood that lay scattered under the snow. Lionel did the same. Then Beatrice produced some matches from her tobacco pouch and lit a small fire.

They huddled next to each other for warmth for most of the night, the cold haunting them into the earliest hours of morning. Lionel stared into the fire, falling in and out of a shivering sleep on Beatrice's shoulder and listening to Ulysses, who stood over them in the darkness. Hunger gnawed at Lionel's stomach, and he thought about the meals they had missed by running away from the school. Lionel knew that Beatrice must be hungry too, but she hadn't said anything, so Lionel didn't say anything either.

The snow continued to fall, wet on their clothes, and Beatrice pointed out that this was a good sign, as the army men would have trouble following their tracks.

"Where are we going?" Lionel asked.

"I figured we'd head to Grandpa's, if I can find it."

Lionel thought about the three hawks and the eagle that he and Beatrice had seen the only time he had ever been to his grandfather's house, near the northwest border of the reservation. Lionel could still see the great birds circling overhead, but had trouble picturing his grandfather's face.

"Do you remember going to Grandpa's?" Beatrice asked. She got up, found a rock, and cracked the ice on the small creek.

"Sort of," Lionel answered.

Beatrice lay down in the snow and cupped water by the handful into her mouth. Lionel watched as she washed the dried blood that lined her face from her temple to her neck. Her forehead was cut, and Lionel wished that he had cracked the ice on the trough with his rock before Jenkins had had the chance to do so with Beatrice's head.

Beatrice smashed more ice, then led Ulysses to the hole so he could drink. Lionel joined them, and soon after, they were on the way, riding northwest toward the mountains.

They rode through the morning, Beatrice sitting tall on Ulysses's back, the snow falling around them. Lionel thought that Beatrice seemed different. She was quiet, which was not unusual, but her silence was stronger, almost as if she were more at ease out here on the open plain despite their troubles. He watched her as she scanned the horizon, looking back from time to time to make sure that they were not being followed.

About midmorning they came to a bluff that overlooked a small group of log cabins and a corral. This was the first time that Lionel and Beatrice had ever laid eyes on the two hundred forty acre plot of Big Bull Boss Ribs.

Chapter Six

Corn Poe Boss Ribs • Big Bull • Ham Hock • "They'll hang ya, alright."

Lionel spotted a small boy watching them as they passed. He was squatting out in the high grass that poked through the snow on the far edge of the bluff. Beatrice saw him too, but continued to ride toward the cabin. The boy pulled up his britches and ran after them.

"Hey, Pa, Pa!" the boy yelled as he ran. "Pa, some riders comin'! Pa, there's riders!"

Lionel could tell that this annoyed Beatrice, but she continued to ride toward the cabin, ignoring the trailing child and his yells. Then the largest man that Lionel had ever seen stepped from the door, bending to clear its low frame. He stood around six feet five and weighed up toward three hundred pounds. On his head sat a bowler derby with a cluster of goose feathers trailing off the back brim.

"My name is Corn Poe, if anyone's asking. That there's my pa, Big Bull Boss Ribs, and this here's his place." The small boy, Corn Poe, panted as he ran up behind them. "Just as a word of caution—he's not real fond of trespassers."

Corn Poe Boss Ribs was eleven, but looked to be about seven. He was the ninth of Big Bull's thirteen children and was considered the runt. He was small, had poor lungs, and had been born a month premature, which Big Bull considered to be a bad sign.

As Beatrice and Lionel rode closer to the door, Big Bull finished gnawing on an old ham bone then threw it to a couple of mangy dogs that circled his feet. Big Bull looked the great horse over, which made Lionel feel uncomfortable to say the least. He couldn't help but think that Big Bull might be capable of eating the horse, or maybe even them. Beatrice must have felt the same because she kept them just beyond the edge of Big Bull's reach.

"That's a good-lookin' horse you two be travelin' with there," Big Bull said, scratching his enormous gut. "What'cha doin' way out here on a horse like that?"

"This horse or his origins is of no concern to you," Beatrice replied.

Big Bull looked them over. "I think that you and that there horse would be bringin' trouble to the Boss Ribs, and that sure as hell concerns me."

"We don't want no trouble. Just the way to the Milk River," Beatrice said firmly.

"We're lookin' for our grandpa who lives up that ways," Lionel added, drawing a glare from Beatrice that did not go unnoticed by Big Bull.

A woman Lionel assumed was Big Bull's wife and a few of his other children gathered in the doorway. Lionel was surprised to see that the woman Big Bull kept as his wife was white like the priest and Brothers back at the boarding school. He hoped that Beatrice would ask her for some food, maybe a blanket to drape around their shoulders as they rode.

"Yep, I think that the soldiers would be comin'. Comin' with troubles for the Boss Ribs. You best be movin' on, alright."

Corn Poe reached up and stroked Ulysses's long mane. "Them soldiers come, I betcha they hang ya."

"Hang us?" Lionel asked. "Why would they wanna hang us?"

"Why, for horse thievin'!" Big Bull bellowed. "I doubt that two mangy Injuns such as yerselves got legal claim to a horse like that one yer ridin' on!"

Big Bull's laugh startled Lionel. It sounded as though he might explode like one of the soldiers' cannons.

"They tryin' to break us Blackfeet from horse thievin'. They'll hang ya, alright," Corn Poe chimed in.

"Who asked you anything?" Big Bull said, throwing a second salted ham hock at Corn Poe. It hit him in the head and fell to the snow. But Corn Poe eagerly picked it up and began to gnaw at it much like his father and the circle of dogs at their feet.

"'Us Blackfeet,' he says, you little half-breeded idjit," Big Bull added.

Lionel just looked at the bone.

"Hell, you two will freeze or starve before them soldier boys get ya, I'll bet," Corn Poe said with the bone clutched in his teeth.

Lionel thought about the Frozen Man. He thought about his own feet and his cold, aching toes.

"None of that is of no worry to you," Beatrice said with a gentle nudge to Ulysses's flank. The horse turned toward the side of the house, and Beatrice dug in her heels to continue their journey north.

"Well, you're headin' in the right direction. Just edge away from the sun till just passed midday and you'll hit the Milk. But you best be advised not to bring no troubles onto your grandfather, if he is truly kin to ya."

Beatrice didn't look back.

"And when you're caught and strung up, you didn't hear none of that from me!" Big Bull laughed.

Lionel looked back to the cabin and the Boss Ribs. The whole family was now outside, standing in front of the house staring at them.

"Remember that you didn't hear none from me. . . ." Big Bull's voice trailed off as the two rounded the back of the house. "And if them soldiers ask, I've got a family to worry about, so I'll be sure to tell 'em you were headin' to the Milk!"

Big Bull's laugh continued to echo from the house as they rode on and out of the Boss Ribs' little valley.

CHAPTER SEVEN

A FOLLOWER • KNIFE FIGHT • INTRODUCTIONS

BEATRICE AND Lionel rode north for most of the afternoon, edging toward the west and the afternoon sun. Beatrice didn't say much, so they rode in silence, pondering what Big Bull had said about bringing trouble down onto their grandfather. Lionel knew that they hadn't eaten in over a day and a half now, and that Corn Poe was right; another night or two out in the cold and they would more than likely end up like the Frozen Man.

Lionel noticed that Beatrice looked behind them more frequently than she had before.

"What is it, Beatrice?" Lionel asked, following her gaze to the deserted horizon.

"I think somebody is following us."

Beatrice pulled Ulysses around, and they made a wide circle back in the direction they had just come. They rode to a low depression in the rolling hills and were soon wading through the four feet of snow that the wind had swept into this little wash. Beatrice pulled up on the horse and slipped silently from his back.

"You stay here. If you hear anything, don't wait for me. You ride hard and don't stop till you hit the river. You understand?"

"Don't wait? Where are you going, Beatrice?" But Beatrice was gone.

Lionel sat with his hands on the warmth of Ulysses's flanks. He felt like crying, but thought that Beatrice hadn't cried, and she was just as hungry, just as cold, and she sure hadn't cried when the man with the patch cracked her head on the ice or when the priest ripped her ear.

Lionel circled Ulysses around to face the mountains that loomed in the distance. They were so big they seemed to stand right before them, but Lionel knew better. If that was where they were going, they were in for a long ride.

Suddenly Ulysses's ears shot back. He flared his nostrils.

"What is it? You hear something?" Then Lionel heard it too. It sounded like someone or something was moving in the snow at the top of the gully.

"Beatrice? Beatrice, is that you?" Lionel was shivering.

He turned the horse and saw someone running straight at him. The movement startled Ulysses, who jumped sideways and out from underneath Lionel. Lionel landed in the snow. This time when he looked up to the top of the gully he could see Beatrice. She was closing in on the runner.

"Help! Help!" the runner screamed, but there was no one to come to his aid. Beatrice tackled the runner, and the two rolled to the bottom of the gully, landing in a heap next to Lionel.

"Get offa me you no-good lunatic!" the runner screamed.

Lionel got up and brushed the snow from his face. He recognized the voice. It belonged to Corn Poe Boss Ribs.

"Free my hands, I dare ya!" Corn Poe screeched. "Free my hands less'n you're afraid, afraid to get a whoopin' you'll be hard-pressed to ever forget!"

Beatrice rolled Corn Poe onto his stomach and

shoved his face in the snow.

"What business do ya have followin' us?" Beatrice demanded.

"Get offa me you chicken-livered jack—"

Beatrice interrupted Corn Poe by shoving his face deeper into the snow.

"You're gonna freeze me eyeballs right out of my head, you idjit!" Corn Poe's muffled cries continued.

Beatrice rolled him back over. "Why are you following us?"

"I'll show you if ya just let me up."

Corn Poe's face was red and pieces of ice dripped from his hair, mixing with the steady stream of tears that now poured from his eyes.

"Come on, let me up and I'll show ya," he cried.

Beatrice pulled him to sit in the snow.

"Well, come on, then," Beatrice said.

Corn Poe reached into his jacket and dug around. Lionel saw Corn Poe's hand flash from his pocket and watched as the little boy scrambled to his feet like a madman. He held a small knife out in front of him.

"I'll teach ya to mess with Corn Poe Boss Ribs," he proclaimed and jabbed the knife at Beatrice.

Beatrice moved slightly, and Corn Poe missed.

He stabbed with the knife again, and Beatrice caught his wrist. With little effort, Beatrice knocked the knife from Corn Poe's hand and shoved him back into the snow. Corn Poe collapsed in a pile of tears. He had trouble catching his breath.

"You're lucky I'm all wet and sluggish or you'd be dead!" Corn Poe carried on, reaching back into his coat.

This prompted Beatrice to kick him, but that didn't stop Corn Poe, and his hand now emerged holding the severed half of a large ham bone. The boy is going to try to kill Beatrice with a ham bone, Lionel thought. He couldn't kill her with a knife, and now he is going to try a ham bone. Beatrice and Lionel stepped back, prepared for Corn Poe's next move, but it didn't come.

"I was just trying to help. I followed to give ya this here ham, and then I got lost and now I can't get back, and ya shoved me in the snow!"

Beatrice sat back on her legs, breathing heavily. "You best keep your voice down."

"Why did ya shove me in the snow? Why?" blubbered Corn Poe. "I'm freezing!"

"Hell, you was trying to kill us," Lionel said.

"Not till this jackass tackled me in the snow!"

Beatrice stood up and offered her hand to Corn Poe. Corn Poe took it, and Beatrice pulled him to his feet.

"I'm sorry I tackled you in the snow," Beatrice said.

Corn Poe caught his breath. "I'm sorry I tried to kill ya with my folding knife," he said, holding the ham bone out to Beatrice. "I brought this all that way for ya."

Beatrice nodded toward Lionel, and Corn Poe handed him the ham bone. "I figured you was hungry."

Lionel bit into the salty cold pork and thought that he had never tasted anything so good in all his life. He took a few bites and then handed it to Beatrice, who did the same.

"Thank you," Beatrice said.

The three stood in the snow passing the ham between them.

"What about you? Ya suddenly gone mute or something?" Corn Poe asked, ripping at the last bit of meat that clung to the now naked bone.

"My name is Lionel. Beatrice is my sister."

"Beatrice? Your sister?" Corn Poe stopped

chewing. "I'd never known that in all them clothes. I hope my pa don't get wind of it. Knocked down by a girl! He'll skin me alive!

"Well, girl or no girl, you got lucky on that go-round," Corn Poe went on between his sporadic gnaws. "Like I was sayin', my name's Corn Poe Boss Ribs. That there was our place back in the valley. My father would kill me if he knew I gave you that ham hock. He hates Injuns, despitin' the fact that he is one."

Corn Poe handed the bone back to Lionel. "But, I must confess, I don't care much how mad he gets. I felt like stretchin' my legs anyhow."

"Well, thanks," Beatrice said again as she walked over to calm Ulysses. "I guess for tonight, Corn Poe, you best be coming with us. Otherwise you'll freeze."

"Freeze? Hell, I'm half frozed as it is."

Beatrice gave Corn Poe back his knife and helped him and Lionel up onto the horse. "Besides, I'd bet you'd be lost before we cleared the next hill," Beatrice teased as she swung up behind them.

"Now, what's that supposed to mean?" Corn Poe shot back.

Beatrice ignored him, and the three rode out of the gully, resuming their course toward the river.

CHAPTER EIGHT

THE COLD • ANTLERS • A MYSTERIOUS VISITOR

THEY RODE the rest of the afternoon, Corn Poe rambling on about everything under the sun and then some. Lionel had never heard anyone who could talk so much, and he soon found himself drifting in and out of sleep as he rocked across the open prairie, riding on the great horse between Corn Poe and Beatrice.

It was the warmest Lionel had been since he had woken the other morning listening to the drip of the melting icicle. Ice didn't seem to be melting now; if anything, Lionel thought that the air had grown colder. Corn Poe must have agreed because he now rode along in silence, slumped forward and buried in Ulysses's mane. Corn Poe could have been dead for all Lionel knew.

Lionel looked down at the snow that passed beneath them and at Corn Poe's leg dangling from the frayed cuff of the small boy's patched work pants. Lionel thought his exposed skin looked almost blue. Blue, like the Frozen Man.

Thinking about the Frozen Man sent a shudder down Lionel's spine. He ran his fingers across the bear claws in his pocket and thought that if he and Beatrice and Corn Poe didn't get wherever they were going soon, they would all be dead, dead like the Frozen Man.

"You cold?" Beatrice asked over the steady cadence of Ulysses's heavy breathing.

"No, I'm okay," Lionel lied.

"How much farther?" Corn Poe moaned.

Good, Lionel thought. Corn Poe isn't dead. Lionel didn't want to see any more dead people.

Lionel scanned the horizon and the rolling hills that rose and fell in the distance with greater frequency. He remembered the pictures of the ships that the captain back at the school had shown him, and thought that the hills looked like the barreling waves of water that the tall ships sailed across. The three of them and Ulysses were like a ship rolling along on a sea of endless snow. Up and down, down and up . . .

"I don't mean to complain, but I don't feel my legs no more," Corn Poe announced.

They had reached the Milk River hours ago. Then, they had continued toward the setting sun. Excluding the occasional clump of cottonwood, they hadn't seen anything but snow in a long time. Lionel thought that it was as if the entire world had stopped, and it was just Lionel, his sister, and the horse . . . and now, Corn Poe.

"Maybe we should walk awhile. Give Ulysses a rest." Beatrice pulled the horse to a stop and slid gracefully from his back. Corn Poe did the same, but his legs gave out and he fell with a plop into a deep snowdrift.

"Boy howdy, this is some of the coldest snow I ever laid eyes on!" Corn Poe proclaimed as he struggled to his feet. He stood there a minute shivering, trying to get the feeling back in his legs.

Lionel slid down and once again scanned the horizon. The past two days raced through his mind, and as he looked around at the snow-covered desolation, he felt again as if he wanted to cry.

"We best keep movin'," Beatrice said.

"How are you plannin' on leadin' that horse without no rope?" Corn Poe asked as he made his way out of the snowdrift.

"He'll follow." And with that, Beatrice continued. As she walked, Ulysses followed. Horses loved Beatrice and Beatrice loved horses, that much Lionel knew—and now so did Corn Poe.

They walked on, but this proved to be harder than they thought. Ulysses's long legs stepped in and out of the snow with ease compared to the children's shorter legs. They were soon warmer from the movement, but exhausted.

"Damn, I'm hungry," Corn Poe exclaimed between gasps. He began to look worried and, like Lionel, could have very well been on the verge of tears.

The three struggled up a high riverbank, with Ulysses fighting his way through the snow behind them. When they got to the top of the rise, Lionel thought he saw something moving toward them from the direction of the river. He strained his eyes and saw it again, this time briefly standing on top of the next bluff. It seemed to Lionel that it was a deer with very large antlers looking at them, almost spying on them. Lionel would catch a glimpse, but then it would disappear only to reappear a few feet from where it last appeared, depending on the direction the children moved. Lionel turned and saw that Beatrice had also seen the strange deer in the distance.

Corn Poe continued, oblivious to the foreign presence, "Y'all remember when I said I needed to stretch my legs? Well, I reckon they are permanently stretched after this one. . . ."

Beatrice raised a finger to her lips, and Corn Poe's eyes went wide.

"What? What is it?" Corn Poe whispered. Lionel couldn't tell if he was shaking from the cold or trembling with fear.

"Lionel, listen to me. You two stay here. Stand next to Ulysses, all right? Just stand there behind him and don't move." And then Beatrice was gone.

Beatrice was fast, and if it weren't for the tracks that she left in the snow behind her, Corn Poe and Lionel might have thought that she just vanished. With his gaze, Lionel traced his sister's tracks as they disappeared down the other side of the gully toward the river. He wanted to follow but knew that Beatrice would not stand for that. Something in the way that she had told Corn Poe and Lionel to stay put kept them right where they were.

"What is it?" Corn Poe asked. His lips were now as blue as his legs.

"We saw something. Something over the hill."

"What in the hell was it? I didn't see nothin'."

"It looked like a deer to me, but we best keep from talkin'," Lionel answered.

"A deer?" Corn Poe exclaimed, louder than Lionel thought he meant to. "You think we might get us some supper after all?"

Corn Poe's comment about supper hit Lionel like a punch in his empty stomach. He glanced up to the ridge, and there it was again not thirty paces away from them—the antlers, at least. This time the antlers did not disappear but seemed to grow. They were getting closer.

Now Corn Poe saw the antlers. Lionel raised his finger to his lips, but with little result.

"What is that?" Corn Poe said, forgetting to whisper altogether. "That don't look like no deer to me!"

It no longer looked like a deer to Lionel either. As it got closer, it began to look more and more like the body of a man with a deer's head. That was about all that Corn Poe needed to see or could stand. He turned in the opposite direction of the ghostly deer-headed creature and moved as fast as he could through the deep snow.

Lionel was tempted to do the same, but given how little distance Corn Poe was gaining and the adamant instructions from Beatrice, he opted to say put. The figure raised its arms into the air, causing Corn Poe to let out a yelp that would raise the dead.

Then the creature began to speak. . . .

"Ássa und! Póóhsapoot!"

But it spoke in a tongue that neither Corn Poe nor Lionel could understand. Lionel spun around, startling Ulysses.

Corn Poe hadn't made it ten steps when he turned back to Lionel. "Come on, ya idjit! It's gonna kill us!"

Lionel took a few steps back, frantically looking around for Beatrice. No Beatrice. He continued to backpedal as the creature moved down the slope toward them. It spoke again, and although its words sounded familiar, Lionel could not understand what it was saying. Then suddenly, it spoke English.

"Don't be afraid, little one. I'm not here to hurt you," the creature called.

Lionel found this hard to believe. As it came closer, it became apparent that the creature was definitely some sort of man, but with the deer head it was about the size of Corn Poe's father, Big Bull.

"Cover your ears! Even the sound of its voice could curse ya for life!" Corn Poe screamed as he crawled though the snow behind Lionel. "It's an apparition, I tell ya! A ghost!"

Lionel believed him. The creature didn't have

trouble in the snow like Lionel and Corn Poe; as a matter of fact, it seemed to float.

"Hey, I told ya, I ain't gonna hurt ya," the deer head called out again. Its voice seemed old and cracked.

"How do we know you're telling the truth? Ghostly apparitions from beyond ain't known for honesty!" Corn Poe yelled, struggling through the snow.

Lionel turned. "How would you know?"

"I know! I saw the spirits when my kid sister Viola died! Run!" Corn Poe was out of breath and barely moving. He seemed to be making his situation worse, and Lionel thought he would soon bury himself alive. Where was Beatrice?

The creature continued down the hill toward them. Lionel decided to make a stand. He crawled through the snowdrift back to Ulysses's side, back to where Beatrice had told him to stay. He studied the creature as it came closer and concluded that although it was strange, it wasn't a ghost. For starters, Lionel realized that it was not floating above the snow, but wore snowshoes that enabled it to skim easily across the top.

"What in the hell are you children doing way out here in weather like this, anyhow?" the deer head asked, now just ten paces away.

"That ain't no concern of yours!" Corn Poe yelled from his snow hole. He was no longer moving and lay panting in the drift.

"It's getting colder and colder, and here y'all are just out wandering?" the deer head continued. "I'd say that the storm pushed through, but another one's on the way. Helluva time for a stroll."

Lionel moved closer and saw that the deer head was actually a hood—a hood worn by an old man. The cowl covered the sides of his face and was fashioned from hide and antlers to mimic a deer's head. Beneath the hood, his face was dark with deep creases around his eyes and mouth. Two thick braids with feathers woven into them fell onto his broad shoulders.

"Well, what's it going to be? You gonna run off like your friend over there and hide in a hole like a rabbit, or are ya gonna stand up and tell me what the hell you're doing out here? Out here on my land?"

Lionel stood perfectly still.

"What—your tongue froze to the roof of your mouth?"

"No—no, sir. We're out here looking . . ."

"Looking for what?" the man demanded.

"Well, I—" Lionel was interrupted as Ulysses's ears shot back, and the big horse let out a long, hard whinny. The noise startled Lionel and caused the old man with the deer-antler hood to spin around—and face Beatrice.

Beatrice sat on the back of a large mule. Lionel had never been so happy to see his sister in all his life.

"Say there, just what do you think you're doing?" the man yelled, pulling a large pistol from beneath his heavy coat.

Before he knew what he was doing, Lionel lunged at the man and the gun. "That's just my sister, don't shoot!" Lionel screamed. He hit the old man as hard as he could, but the man easily held him off with his free hand, aiming the pistol at Beatrice.

"If you know what's good for ya, you'll step down from my mule!"

But Beatrice didn't get down from the mule. She chose instead to spur the animal forward and slowly ride it down the snowy slope toward Lionel, the man with the hood, and Ulysses.

"I knew this would come to no good!" Corn Poe yelled from his hole.

The man seemed puzzled and unsure how to react to Beatrice's icy defiance. Beatrice continued forward, and Lionel saw that the mule pulled a travois, and on that sled was the carcass of a small elk.

Beatrice rode right up to them and slid effortlessly from the back of the mule to Ulysses. She then handed the man the mule's reins. He watched Beatrice, a puzzled look still on his face.

"Beatrice?" the man stuttered in disbelief, then spun to face Lionel. "So . . . you're Lionel. I should have seen it in your eyes. I'm slippin' in my old age, I tell ya."

Lionel looked up at Beatrice, who sat calmly on Ulysses's back. Beatrice might have been a girl, Lionel thought, but she sure looked like a warrior up there on that great horse.

"Why, this is a surprise! Beatrice, it's been a while, and you . . ." the man said as he roughly shook Lionel's half-frozen hand, "when I last saw you, hell if you weren't but two foot tall. I'm your grandpa."

His grandfather's hand felt warm as it engulfed his.

"Why, judgin' from yer hand, you're half froze, boy."

Lionel heard the word "froze" and instinctively slipped his other hand in his coat pocket, feeling the Frozen Man's bear claws.

"We better get you out of this weather," their grandfather continued. "I tell ya, another storm's coming."

Beatrice and Lionel's grandpa pulled his mule's reins tight and circled back to the small hill.

"We ain't too far from my place, so I think it's best we get going. We can talk there. I'll be interested to hear what y'all are doin' way out here and where you got that horse you're on there, Beatrice."

In a few steps, their grandfather was halfway up the hill.

"And you best fetch your rabbit friend over there. He might be interested to see how us ghosts are livin' in this here modern age."

CHAPTER NINE

A BELLY FULL • RECOUNTING THE ESCAPE • BUFFALO ROBE • NAPI THE OLD MAN • LIONEL'S DREAM

THE FIRE in Grandpa's cabin on the Milk River danced around the cast-iron cauldron that hung in the stone fireplace.

"There's more stew in there, boy," Grandpa reminded Lionel as he threw a small piece of birch wood onto the fire.

A strong north wind whipped at the tiny cabin, a last-ditch effort to extend winter just one storm longer. Lionel was tired, and his stomach had never been this full.

Corn Poe slept next to Lionel, and from the sound of his snoring, slept soundly. The small boy hadn't moved since he had finished his third helping of stew and collapsed in front of the fire, rubbing his thin, pale legs. Now Lionel lay wrapped in a thick buffalo robe, listening to Corn Poe's heavy, labored breathing and Beatrice's retelling of their escape from the boarding school and the soldiers' outpost. It had all happened so fast.

As Beatrice told of the Frozen Man and how the soldiers had laughed and stolen from him, Grandpa's face looked first sad and then angry. But he didn't say anything. Not a word.

Beatrice went on about the priest, and that all she wanted to do was to pray like her mother used to. Beatrice told Grandpa that she wanted to learn these prayers, not the prayers that the government made for them. Then Beatrice told Grandpa about Sergeant Haskell Jenkins and Private Samuel Lumpkin and how they held her under the freezing water and tried to cut her hair with the sheep shears.

Lionel stared at the fire, but all he could see was Jenkins's snarling smirk and the darker-than-midnight black leather of his coarse eye patch.

Beatrice told Grandpa how she drove the sheep shears through Jenkins's hand and that she was worried because she did not feel bad about it . . . not in the least. She told him that Jenkins deserved it and she would do it again, or worse, if given the opportunity. Then Beatrice told Grandpa about Lionel, and Ulysses the great horse.

Grandpa leaned over and smoothed Lionel's hair with his big hand. Lionel felt happy wrapped in the buffalo robe, lying before the fire with a belly full of food, listening to his sister. But Lionel also had a feeling that everything had suddenly changed.

Grandpa sat back in his rocking chair by the fire to pack and light his pipe.

"Well, the government can't be too happy. I wonder how long it will take them to figure out that you'd come and try to find me," Grandpa said after a while. "The snow helps, but they're coming."

Grandpa took a long draw on his pipe. He released a swirl of smoke that hung in the rafters. "They are definitely coming."

"I'm sorry, but let 'em come," Beatrice said almost without emotion. "They can't catch me. I'm never going back."

Grandpa took another draw; Lionel and Beatrice listened to the low crackling burn of its embers. Rings of smoke followed and drifted about the room amid the fire's dancing light.

Lionel shifted and felt the bear claws dig into his side. He was ashamed to show them to anyone, but wondered if his grandfather could tell him if the Frozen Man might need the claws wherever it was he had gone.

Lionel broke the silence. "Grandpa?"

"Yes, Lionel?"

"Where did the Frozen Man go?"

"Where did he go?" their grandfather asked, leaning farther back in his rocker.

"Yes, I don't understand. At the school they said that—"

"Ah well, at school," Grandpa interrupted, "people say a lot of things; and me, I wouldn't even know where to start."

"At the beginning," Lionel answered.

"Listen to him, will you?" Their grandfather laughed, exhaling a large cloud from his pipe. "It's a long story, but maybe you're right. To get to the end, it just might be better to start at the beginning."

Lionel lost his grandfather's face for a moment in the smoke.

"But this was a long time ago. Back in the days of Napi, Napi the Old Man."

"Napi?" Beatrice asked, pushing the hair out of her eyes.

Their grandfather hesitated. "It's late. You two should sleep and let me think about what has happened."

Beatrice watched their grandfather with a solemn expression on her face. He shifted uncomfortably.

"Okay, okay, but just for a bit, now. You two need to join your friend there and get some sleep."

The children lay back in front of the fire.

"From the start. Way back, eh? Let's see," their grandfather began, "when I was a boy, the old ones used to say that there was a time when everything, this whole world, was covered with water. This was before the time of this land."

Lionel stared into the dancing firelight, trying to imagine what it would be like to ride a horse under that much water.

"Waves rose and fell, crashed and churned, but nothing . . . only water." Their grandfather sat forward with a creak of his rocker. "Well, almost nothing.

"Way out, in the midst of this vast sea, there was a raft and there was an Old Man on the raft—well, a

Spirit, really, a powerful Spirit. The Spirit's name was Napi, and he spent his days picking up various animals that had been left to fend for themselves across the great floods.

"One day Napi saw that he had collected many animals and that the raft was crowded. He thought that he must find a place where they could all live, so he told the Beaver to swim down to the bottom and bring him some mud. Napi thought that he could use the mud to make some land. So, the Beaver dove into the swirling waters.

"The Beaver was down a long time but then burst to the surface, gasping for breath. 'No matter how deep . . . no matter how hard I swam . . . I could not reach the bottom,' he panted.

"The Old Man then sent the Loon, then the Otter, but the water was still too deep. Napi asked all of the animals, 'Do any of you think that you can reach the bottom?' All the animals were silent, all except for a small Muskrat."

Lionel looked over at Corn Poe with heavy-lidded eyes.

"'I will dive to the bottom and bring back the mud to you,' the Muskrat announced.

"'You?' asked the Beaver. The Muskrat answered by diving off the raft and into the deep water.

"The Muskrat was also gone for a long time. The Old Man figured he must'a drowned, but just when the Old Man had given up all hope, the Muskrat appeared, floating, just about dead, on the horizon. The Old Man pulled the tiny Muskrat onto the raft and saw that there was mud between his claws. The Muskrat had made it to the bottom.

"Napi dried the mud from the Muskrat's paw and spread it across the surface of the water, and there, land was formed. So, Old Man and the animals said goodbye to the raft and traveled across the land, the Old Man creating things as he saw fit. He told the rivers where to run and the trees, bushes, and flowers where they should grow. He carried with him a pocketful of boulders and stones so that he could build the mountains. He told the grass to grow on the plains, and the berries and roots to grow by the rivers."

Lionel felt his eyes closing. His grandfather's voice sounded more distant.

"When the Old Man was done, he gathered the animals and told them, 'Go live on this land. Drink from these rivers and eat this grass, these berries and roots.'

"The animals thanked the Old Man and did as he asked them to do. Some of the animals went to the rolling prairie and some to the mountains . . ."

Lionel fell asleep dreaming that he stood on the edge of the plains, a great woods at his back. The prairie now churned in a sea of swirling grass before him. He looked from the woods to a small raft as it crested a distant wave out on the rolling hills. Corn Poe, Beatrice, and his grandfather were on the raft, drifting farther and farther away from Lionel; drifting and soon disappearing to somewhere on the far side of the horizon.

CHAPTER TEN

EARLY MORNING • BEATRICE'S FEATHER • SUPPLIES • CORN POE'S DEPARTURE • LISTEN

LIONEL WOKE to the sound of Corn Poe's voice.

"Hell, I may have to grow my hair out," Corn Poe said. "Then you could wrap mine just like that."

Lionel lifted the heavy buffalo robe and sat up. His body was stiff, but he felt rested and somehow, once again hungry. He turned to see Beatrice sitting on the corner of the fireplace and Grandpa still in his rocker by her side.

Beatrice looked different. She looked more like Grandpa than she had when Lionel had fallen asleep. Strips of red and blue flannel were woven into her long, thick braids, and one of their grandfather's hunting knives hung from a beaded belt that was cinched at her waist. Lionel wondered if perhaps his dream were true and that Beatrice had changed on the far side of the horizon, and then returned.

"I'll lend you this until you and young Lionel there find your own way," Grandpa was saying as he tied a long feather from a red-tailed hawk's wing into Beatrice's braid.

Beatrice smiled, and Lionel thought that it was the first time he had seen her smile since before they had left the boarding school. Lionel ran his hand across his closely cropped hair.

"Don't you worry. You're next. It just might take a while before we can get to it, eh, boy?" Grandpa stood to stoke the coals from the previous night. "I think we best get moving."

Lionel saw through the cabin's small frosted windows that it was still dark. He slipped back into his clothes and crossed to the door.

"Get some water on your way back," Grandpa called after Lionel. "It's good to see you up on your feet. I was beginning to wonder if you would ever wake."

Lionel smiled, opened the cabin's door, and stepped out onto the fresh-fallen snow. He stood for a moment looking up at the faded stars and full moon that still hung in the far corners of the clear, early-morning sky. The air was cold and dry, and Lionel could feel it filling his lungs as he walked past the small stable to the outhouse.

Ulysses stood in a stall next to Grandpa's mule. He snorted to the air as Lionel passed.

"I'll get to you, don't worry about that," Lionel said, his voice cracking with his first words of the day.

Lionel continued to the outhouse, looking to the river, confused by what his grandfather had told him about Napi the Old Man creating the land. The Brothers and priest at the school had told Lionel that the world, the entire world, was created by someone else, not Napi the Old Man, and that it had taken six days. He wondered how two different people could create the same world on which they walked and rode across every day. He still wondered what had happened to the Frozen Man.

When Lionel retuned to the warmth of the cabin, he heard the snap, popping sound of bacon. Corn Poe sat by the fire with a long fork in his hand.

"Hey, there. That's for all of us," Grandpa shouted

across the room as Corn Poe tried to blow on a piece of sizzling bacon that was already in his mouth.

Grandpa stood over a wooden table with Beatrice at his side, looking at a large map. "The river will lead you up into the Mountain, but remember there are many twists and turns. Once you get to the base of the Mountain, a stream will join the river. You must follow this stream north. The stream will take you to the valley and then the meadow."

Lionel glanced around the room. Small bundles made of heavy canvas lay about in preparation for travel. There was grain for Ulysses, a collection of small pots and pans, preserved vegetables in glass jars, canned fruit, salt pork, jerked venison, and various items of heavy wool clothes. The buffalo robe that Lionel slept in was also tied into a tight bundle and sitting next to the supplies.

"Where are we going?" Lionel asked.

"Into the Mountain," Grandpa replied, and went about his work.

They ate a large breakfast of eggs, slab bacon, and canned pears; then Grandpa told Lionel to go out and tend to Ulysses because they had a long ride ahead of them.

Lionel stepped back out into the morning thinking about what his grandfather said. Into the Mountain? Where was that?

Lionel could see the first hints of light in the eastern sky. He fed Ulysses, then led him to the river where the great horse drank. Lionel scanned the horizon, hoping to catch a glimpse of the three hawks and the eagle that circled his memory of their grandfather's cabin, but the sky was empty except for the low snow clouds that hung in the distance.

Lionel turned back to the cabin and wondered if, wherever they were headed, he would ever see Grandpa's place again. He hoped that if he did return, he could come live with Grandpa instead of at the boarding school. Lionel liked school but thought that living with his grandfather would be better and something that, at the very least, he should try. He thought about what his sister had said and felt that he too would like to learn about the ways of the Old People.

Lionel's thoughts were interrupted by Grandpa, Beatrice, and Corn Poe, who gathered with the bundles around Ulysses. Grandpa instructed Beatrice how to tie the supplies to the back of the horse. Then he handed her a long rifle wrapped in buckskin and a wooden box filled with ammunition.

"I want you to be careful with this. Kill only what you'll eat."

Corn Poe stood back, inspecting the horse and its newly configured load. The small boy was quiet this morning, and Lionel thought that the cold must be taking its toll on him.

"I don't see how we're all gonna fit with all this here junk you got tied all over," Corn Poe said, more to Grandpa than anyone else.

"You're right about that. I think you'll be coming with me," Grandpa said as he double-checked the lashings. "We'll wander for a while to throw off them government boys, and then I'll get you back to your home."

"But . . . I thought . . ." Corn Poe stammered.

"Well, you thought wrong. It's too cold to be wanderin' about unless you have to. Until we straighten this all out, these two don't have a choice. You do, and I'm making it for you," Grandpa said with a wink. "Besides, we're on a mission of our own."

Grandpa spun Ulysses around and lifted Lionel onto his back. Lionel's legs were stiff, as if he'd just gotten off the horse moments before.

"Now, me and the Corn Poe's wanderin' won't throw them for long, but it should help. You're going to need every little bit of a lead we can give. Hell, to be honest with ya, if you can make it to the Mountain, I doubt you'll see any of them soldiers until well into the thaw. Maybe not even till summer."

Beatrice slipped up behind Lionel, and Grandpa threw the buffalo robe around them.

"Now, Beatrice, it might be cold out there in the open, but I want you to walk in the shallows of the river when you can for the first half of the day. It'll be harder for them to track you from the river, and this big fellow looks like he can handle it."

Grandpa slipped a rawhide harness over Ulysses's head.

"From the looks of things, you should get some more snow this afternoon. That'll help. You hide out until you hear from me. I'll bring this one back by the Boss Ribs' place and see what I can find out, and then, once some of the excitement has worn off, I'll come and find ya with more supplies and some sorta plan."

Beatrice took the reins in her hands and turned Ulysses toward the river.

"Now, I want you two to pay attention. Be aware of what's around you and watch. That school and them government men tried to kill that in ya. You've got to find and listen to it. Listen to the animals, the wind, the mountains. We may not speak the same language no more, but they're talkin' to ya. It's up to you if you choose to listen."

Grandpa took a long braid of twisted sweet grass from his jacket and lit the end. He raised it high above his head and began to sing. The smoke swirled above him and lay flat on the cold morning air. Corn Poe stood at his side watching Grandpa's every move as Beatrice urged Ulysses past them and into the shallow icy water of the river.

Chapter Eleven

An Icy River • Old Man Makes People • Leaving the Reservation • Lionel's Second Dream

Ulysses struggled as they navigated their way along the river's icy banks. The riverbed consisted of large loose rocks that caused the horse to slip and stumble, and Beatrice and Lionel had to stop twice to retie the load.

As they rode, Beatrice recounted what their grandfather had told her during the night after Lionel had fallen asleep. She told Lionel that a long time ago, their grandfather had been made to join the government's army, and that he had been taken by a large boat across a great body of water where they fought other men who spoke different languages. Many men died, including two of Grandpa's older brothers.

They gave Grandpa a medal like the ones the captain wore, but Grandpa didn't want it. He thought that it was given to him because he had somehow survived while so many others were killed. Grandpa buried the medal for his brothers on the banks of the river.

As they rode, the mountains got closer and closer, and Lionel thought that they might reach them that very afternoon, but he was wrong.

Midday, as Grandpa had said, a stream joined the river. Beatrice led Ulysses up onto a sandy snow-covered bank of the tributary, where they stopped to rest and eat. They ate cold elk meat and some of the hardtack biscuits that their grandfather had packed for them, and then were back on their way.

As they rode through the afternoon, Beatrice told Lionel more about Napi the Old Man, as their grandfather had explained it to her.

"Grandpa said that after the Old Man created the world, he realized that he was lonely and that he needed someone to talk to. So one day the Old Man decided that it was time to create people—us, I reckon. The Old Man made two figures of clay, one of a woman and one of her son. The Old Man buried 'em in the ground by the river and left 'em."

"Why would he leave them?"

Beatrice stared at him blankly, then continued, "The Old Man returned on the second day and noticed that the clay figures had changed but still didn't look like people. On the third day, he came back and once again, although they were different, they still weren't people. On the fourth day, Grandpa said that the Old Man returned and unburied 'em. He told the clay people to get up and walk; and they did . . ."

"They did?" Lionel asked, turning to look at Beatrice.

"Yup. 'Cause now they were people."

"How did that happen?"

"I don't know," Beatrice answered. "Grandpa didn't say."

Lionel surveyed the vast landscape and the approaching foothills of the mountains. The land slowly changed as Beatrice spoke. The rolling plains gave way to foothills. The foothills grew bigger and seemed to sprout clumps of trees, mostly pine, aspen, and birch.

"Grandpa said that the Old Man led the clay people to the water at the edge of the river where he told them, 'I am Napi. Napi the Old Man.' But the Old Man knew that like him, the people would be lonely, so he took more clay and blew onto it. The clay became more men and women, but now the Old Man figured that his people were hungry, and they didn't have no clothes. So he took more clay and made the buffalo. He told the clay people that the buffalo and the other animals were their food, and told them to hunt 'em."

Lionel thought about Napi the Old Man building the mountains and telling the plants where to grow. Then he thought about the clay people and the buffalo.

Sometime late that afternoon the children reached the dilapidated remnants of a barbed wire fence that Beatrice, although unsure, figured to be the boundary of their reservation. Neither Lionel nor Beatrice had ever left the reservation. Lionel was not sure if the same could be said about Ulysses.

They paused before the fence and marveled as it snaked north and south as far as their eyes could see. Lionel looked across the fence and thought that besides the proximity of the looming mountains, the rough terrain looked remarkably similar to the land that they had traveled for the majority of the afternoon.

Beatrice seemed nervous and turned Ulysses in a circle, surveying the snow-covered desolation that surrounded them.

"You think you're ready?" Beatrice asked, breaking the uneasy feeling that the immense border brought.

"I guess" was all Lionel could think to say.

"We may never be coming back, you know. We may never be allowed back," Beatrice added, and then dug in her heels, asking Ulysses to proceed.

The horse stepped forward, and with that step, completely alone and without permission or legal permit, the children rode through a gaping hole in the fence, leaving the reservation and all that they had ever known.

It grew dark, and Beatrice led Ulysses toward a small rock outcrop that jutted up from the bank. That night they slept off the reservation for the first time in their lives, wrapped in the buffalo robe in the shallow of a small cave at the foot of the mountains. They roasted the elk on sticks and ate; then Beatrice lay down and did not move until morning. Lionel wondered how much she had slept the night before.

Lionel fell asleep listening to the crackling embers

of the small fire they had built. He dreamed that he stood on the side of a great river. There, he saw the bighorn sheep, the antelope, and then the buffalo rise from the earth and run across the river and out onto the open rolling plains. Lionel heard a low rumble from the earth, and Beatrice and their grandfather rose from the banks. They also crossed the river and followed the buffalo and the other animals. In his dream, Lionel tried to follow, but could not make it across the great river. The river's opposite bank was moving farther away, moving to well beyond the distant horizon.

CHAPTER TWELVE

BEATRICE GROWS WEARY • COLD AND MORE SNOW • INTO THE MOUNTAINS

WHEN LIONEL woke, Beatrice was still asleep. He lay curled in the buffalo robe next to his sister and thought about the clay people and if they grew to become the Blackfeet. He wondered if the people Napi the Old Man created were the same as the first two people the Brothers and priests at the boarding school had told him were the first created. Their first man had also been created from the earth: the woman from a rib. Lionel concluded that they must have been the first two white people, and that the clay people Grandpa had told Beatrice about were the first of the Blackfeet.

Lionel got up, stoked the fire for Beatrice, and led Ulysses down to the stream to drink. A distant sun stretched across the dull morning sky. Lionel turned with the first light and looked toward the great mountains and the black menacing clouds that clung to their tops. He returned to their camp and found Beatrice rolling up the buffalo robe. She seemed detached and tired, so Lionel lifted the bundles and tied them to Ulysses the way his grandfather had showed him, without speaking.

They ate cold elk and were soon on their way, riding well into the afternoon. They continued to follow the stream, pushing Ulysses up the increasingly rough and rocky terrain and under the long stretches of trees that seemed to touch the sky. They came to several forks in the stream but always kept to the right, fighting the deep banks of snow that lay on either side.

Lionel noticed that the stream grew smaller the higher they traveled, and eventually more difficult to follow. By late afternoon, the only evidence that the river was still with them was the low gurgle of water that struggled unseen under its heavy coat of winter ice and snow.

Sometime late that afternoon, it began to snow again. The snow covered the trees and caused their branches to bend and drop their burden onto the children and the great horse as they passed. Lionel grew cold as the day wore on, and Beatrice pulled the robe tighter. They drifted in and out of sleep, but Beatrice always woke in time to keep Ulysses going or to navigate the river's increasingly treacherous banks.

It soon became dark, but Ulysses continued to climb. Occasionally he would throw back his head or nip gently at the children's feet to wake them, as if he could tell when the children were slipping while they slept. Beatrice began to cough sometime in the night, and Lionel thought about when she had been sick. The captain had told Lionel that it was possible that Beatrice might never be able to leave the infirmary. But Beatrice had showed them. Beatrice always showed them.

The snow stopped falling sometime near morning. Lionel woke and looked above them at the clearing clouds and the ink black night with its sparkling array of stars now clustered overhead. Beatrice continued coughing in her sleep, so Lionel stayed awake, taking in the landscape that surrounded them. Light soon filled the morning sky, revealing a world that was entirely new to him. Lionel had grown accustomed to the wide-open space of the boarding school and the reservation. Here in the mountains, he couldn't see more than a hundred paces before the dense snow-covered trees or large white-dolloped boulders blocked his view. They continued on, and soon Lionel fell back asleep.

CHAPTER THIRTEEN

A CROOKED LODGE • LIONEL TAKES CARE OF BEATRICE • "WE MADE IT"

LIONEL FOUND himself staring into the tangled mess of Ulysses's tousled mane. He looked around, trying to fully wake up and get his bearings. He discovered he was in a small, dilapidated, open-sided barn. Ulysses was tearing at an empty burlap grain sack, attempting to get the last of its remnants into his big mouth. Beatrice was still asleep.

Lionel rubbed his eyes and wondered for a moment if it hadn't all been some kind of dream, and he was actually back at the school about to be in trouble for sitting on Ulysses's back. His body ached, and he was cold.

He crawled from beneath the buffalo robe, carefully, so as not to wake his sister, then dropped to the frozen dirt of the stable and collapsed. Lionel's legs and feet still hadn't woken up. He sat for a minute and saw that Ulysses's deep tracks followed the stream across a small, open, tree-lined meadow. Mountains loomed above them on all sides.

Lionel looked up at his sister. She slumped forward with her arms sprawled across the horse's neck. Lionel had never seen her sleep this much and decided to leave her while he investigated their latest stop.

He left the shelter of the stable and stepped out into the deep snow of the meadow. It came up to his waist, and after only a few steps he had to stop to catch his breath. He had never seen this much snow in his life. Though the surroundings seemed peaceful, he could not shake the feeling that they were not alone. Something was watching them.

Lionel scanned the tree line to find that a large raven, so black it looked almost blue, was sitting opposite him on a spindly winter branch, calmly observing the small valley's newest inhabitants. "Hello," Lionel called, but the bird just spread its large wings and took to the air.

Lionel watched the raven fly its way to the tops

of the nearby trees, but as he did, he caught something else out of the corner of his eye. There, at the far corner of the meadow, nestled back and surrounded by a small stand of pine, birch, and aspen, sat a long, lonely log cabin. Despite its size, Lionel almost missed it, as the building seemed either to have sprung from the earth or to be in the process of being taken back into it.

The chimney stood like a stone giant that had lost its balance, fallen, and then leaned on the lodge, pushing the entire structure to one side and collapsing the roof on the farthest end. The remaining roof was covered by four feet of snow. Lionel thought that it looked like frosting on top of a cake or, more accurately, the frosting on a cake that someone had dropped.

Lionel returned to the stable. Beatrice was still sleeping, so he took Ulysses by his rawhide harness and led them toward the slumping building. Even the doorframe leaned to one side.

He left Beatrice with the horse and pushed open the heavy, crooked door. The door creaked on its leather hinges, revealing, once he was inside, that over half of the building still seemed to be perfectly intact. The other side fell off in a maze of cracked timber and broken glass, but the rubble passed for a fourth wall.

Light from outside shone through the dingy windows, and Lionel already felt a little warmer stepping inside and out of the wind that came down off the mountains and across the small meadow. He made his way around various bits of debris and toward the center of the enormous fireplace. You could have put four of Grandpa's fireplaces into this one, Lionel thought. A box of kindling stood next to the giant stones, and in no time Lionel had a small fire going that was dwarfed by its immense surroundings. Lionel decided that if he could do it, he should bring both Ulysses and Beatrice into the house. How else would he be able to carry his sleeping sister?

It took some coaxing, but he convinced Ulysses to lower his head, and led them both into the cavernous warmth that his little fire and the fallen lodge provided. Lionel did his best to wrap Beatrice in the buffalo robe and lower her gently in front of the fire, but despite his best effort she still tumbled off the horse's back.

Beatrice sat up and looked around. "We made

it," she said, and drifted back to sleep. Though it was frigid out, Lionel thought that Beatrice's face felt hot. But she was shivering, so he got her some water, wrapped the buffalo robe tight, and turned back to stoke the fire.

Lionel led Ulysses to the far side of the lodge, figuring that the horse could sleep there for the night. Ulysses snorted and poked at the cabin's crumbled remains as Lionel did his best to unload their supplies. He located their tight bundles of food, then sat down by the fire next to Beatrice and ate some of the dried meat. He was tired and cold, but as Beatrice said, they had made it.

Part Two

A LARGE man on a big horse stopped suddenly, just as he had made his way through the high pines above the small meadow in the midst of the great mountains. Something was different. It had snowed off and on for the last two days, and now that he had enough pelts and meat, he was looking forward to returning to the small lodge to rest and repair some of the traps that had been damaged over the course of this long winter.

"Smoke, that is what it is, smoke," the man said aloud, a slight Caribbean accent punctuating the word "smoke."

The man dropped back down from the ridge, his horse plowing through the snow and into a small clearing hidden in a large stand of birch and aspen. The man then cupped his hands, raised them to his mouth, and made the call of a barred owl.

He seemed to sing the words "Who? Who? Who cooks for you?" But that was only how it sounded.

A small boy on horseback joined the man. He was trailing two horses that carried loads wrapped in heavy waxed canvas. The boy and the horses seemed to appear from out of the thin mountain air.

"I think it'd be best to keep moving," the man said to the boy. "Looks like someone might be down in the lodge."

The small boy did not reply, but simply stared back at the large man with big dark eyes.

"We'll skip the stop this time and hope they're gone when we get back in a month or so," the man continued. "That fallen cabin sure is pleasant in the springtime."

The boy again did not say a word, but this time replied with a nod.

"Well, it's agreed, then," the man said with a smile, "maybe next month."

The large man and the small boy urged their horses forward and melted into the maze of snow-covered trees that stood before them.

The man's name was Avery John Hawkins. The boy, he was silent.

Chapter Fourteen

Wolverine • A Broken Chair • Ulysses's Wrath • The Hole in the Chimney

Lionel woke to an explosion of commotion. The lodge was filled with low, guttural snarls and the sound of a great collision. Ulysses paced wildly across the back of the room.

"Open the door, maybe he just wants to leave," Beatrice said, her voice calm.

She was no longer sleeping but standing over a large, snarling wolverine, holding it back with the end of a broken broom.

Lionel scrambled to his feet and ran to open the door. The wolverine did not take them up on the invitation.

"Get that broken chair," Beatrice instructed.

Lionel ran back, grabbing the broken pieces of

a fallen chair that lay strewn across the floor. Lionel had seen wolverines before, but he had never seen one this agitated. The dog-sized animal viciously attacked the broom, sending the splintered ends flying across the room.

"The chair, Lionel," Beatrice repeated.

Lionel held the chair out in front of him like the lion tamer from the traveling circus that had stopped by the boarding school one summer. The wolverine turned its focus to Lionel, swatting at the chair's legs with its long claws, practically pulling it from his hand.

"Start moving him toward the door," Beatrice said as she ran to the other side of the room, returning with a long stool.

They backed the animal slowly toward the door, Lionel using every bit of strength that he could muster to keep the wolverine from knocking the chair from his hand—or worse, getting past it.

He took his eyes from the wolverine for a moment as they pushed the snarling beast past the bundled supplies. Lionel saw their grandfather's rifle and wondered why Beatrice didn't use it. When he looked back from the rifle a second later, the wolverine

splintered the chair and swiped at Lionel's leg with a powerful swoop of its long claws.

Lionel felt the creature's paw take his legs out from under him. Before he could move, Beatrice was in between the wolverine and Lionel, pushing the creature back with the stool. She stood close to the open doorway, but the wolverine refused to leave.

Lionel glanced down at his leg. Four long lines of blood appeared on the leg of his torn long underwear. He looked at the wolverine and thought that it might kill them.

Lionel grabbed his lower leg and pulled himself back toward Ulysses, who kicked and bucked wildly toward Beatrice and the wolverine. Beatrice looked over her shoulder and jumped out of the way as one of Ulysses's kicks came dangerously close. The wolverine did the same, twisting sideways in the crooked doorframe and then flattening itself to the ground to avoid another powerful kick. Beatrice seized the opportunity, sprang to her feet, and pushed the door closed on the wolverine. She then dropped the door's wooden latch to secure it.

The wolverine clawed and scratched at the worn wood, sending splintered pieces through the exposed cracks. Beatrice leaned on the door with all of her weight until the wolverine realized that she was not going to let it through. Lionel sat up, and through the dingy windows saw the still-snarling animal slowly waddle through the windblown drifts of snow. Lionel looked down at his leg again, and then fell back against their bundles of supplies.

"I don't think that the wolverine liked us in his house," Beatrice said as she knelt at Lionel's side. "It looks like he got ya."

"Just a bit, eh?" Lionel said, trying to be brave.

"Yeah, just a bit," Beatrice replied, pulling up the leg of his long underwear. "I'll get some soap and water on it, and it should be all right. We did pretty good, huh—I mean all of us?" Beatrice reached up and scratched Ulysses's long face.

"Yeah, Beatrice, pretty good," Lionel said, as the pain slowly drifted up his leg.

Beatrice wet the end of Lionel's torn underwear and wiped the blood away. "The good news is that it ain't all that deep," she said, "and now you're a part of that wolverine forever."

"How do you figure?" Lionel asked.

"Well, you ain't never gonna forget it. You'll have yerself that scar as a reminder," Beatrice said as she dabbed at the cuts with a torn piece of cloth.

"How did he get in here?" Lionel asked, looking anxiously around the room.

"I don't know. I heard something. Sat up, and he was there," Beatrice said, looking over toward the hulking pile of the chimney's stacked rock. Then she noticed something and got up to investigate.

"Oh, I see. Look, look here. There's a hole."

Lionel crawled to his feet, and limped over to Beatrice at the chimney. There in the side of the crumbling pile of stone was a large crack that he hadn't seen when he had first found the lodge.

"It must have happened when the chimney fell forward, huh?" Lionel said.

"Yeah, I guess so, and now we ruined his hiding place," Beatrice said. "He'll be all right, now that winter's about over."

Lionel looked out the grimy window at the freshly fallen snow that surrounded their new home.

"How's the leg?" Beatrice asked.

"I think it will be all right," Lionel answered. "You okay? You sure got sleepy."

"I'm better now, I just get tired," Beatrice said, and they both collapsed in a pile on the buffalo robe in front of the fire.

"I'm going to think about that wolverine," Lionel said. "Like Grandpa told us."

"Grandpa?" Beatrice asked.

"Yeah. I'm tryin' to keep my eyes open and listen," Lionel said again, more to himself this time.

Chapter Fifteen

Sleep • Silk Gowns and Top Hats • The Meadows' Green • The Great Wood • Surprise

Beatrice and Lionel slept on and off for the next few days, taking turns getting water from the stream, stoking the fire, and preparing small meals from the provisions that their grandfather sent with them. Once rested, Beatrice thought that they should assess the cabin for additional supplies, and upon further investigation Lionel discovered an old trunk and a phonograph under the rubble at the far end of the lodge.

The children had never seen a phonograph or the hard wax cylinders that were labeled "Edison Gold Moulded Records" that accompanied the machine. It took the children the better part of a morning to figure out how to work the apparatus, but when they did, they were grateful that Edison, whoever he was, had left the cylinders for their enjoyment.

The trunk had long since been scavenged for anything of real use but still held an eclectic assortment of moldy silk gowns and a coat with long tails. Beatrice took to wearing a dress of ivory silk and pearl buttons, Lionel a long coat and a hat whose crown looked liked the cylinders that spun the music. The late-winter days were perfect for dressing up and then dancing to the scratchy sounds of Edison's collection. Beatrice was happy, as happy as Lionel remembered ever seeing her. And Beatrice was right about the snow; although it was still freezing at night, the days were sunny and the snow was melting.

At the start of the third week in the lodge, Beatrice tore her ivory gown while cutting wood. She referred to the frock as "stupid," and returned to the faded blues of her dated school uniform.

"I'm wondering how long our supplies will last," Beatrice mused as she folded the torn garment.

Lionel turned from the hearth, where he held the last of the elk that their grandfather had given them over the fire. Beatrice looked concerned.

"How long do we stay?" he asked.

And then it dawned on him. How long were they planning on staying? When was Grandpa coming? Lionel had never thought about it. Jenkins and Lumpkin had been trying to drown Beatrice, and then they ran. They had never made a plan. It just worked. Or had so far. Now, Beatrice was worried about the supplies.

Beatrice decided that they should go hunting, but just in the immediate area around the lodge. Although a lot of the snow had melted and there were patches of green grass and saturated moss across the meadow, they thought that they should stay close to the lodge until they heard from their grandfather.

The next day Beatrice loaded the rifle, and they went out across the meadow to the edge of the woods. Trees spiraled above them, and Lionel felt a stillness to the place that reminded him of the chapel back at school. For some reason, once they were in these great woods, they spoke only in whispers.

Lionel walked behind Beatrice, doing his best to stay within her exact footsteps. The ground was thick with a thousand years and a thousand layers of the giant trees. Moss-covered branches and rotting trunks of all shapes and sizes lay scattered like discarded bones around the ancient trunks that towered high above their heads. They saw two deer, a rabbit, and some squirrels, and although Beatrice fired twice, they would return to the lodge empty-handed.

They walked back without speaking, Lionel wondering how Beatrice had missed the animals. He tried to remember the last time he had seen Beatrice fail at anything. Then Beatrice froze.

Lionel watched as her eyes went wide and swept the high trees.

"What is it?" Lionel whispered.

"There's someone else in the woods."

Lionel did not hear anything except for the wind in the tops of the trees, the distant murmur of the stream, and their own uneven breathing. Beatrice crept forward. Lionel closed his eyes and tried to lower the creaking groan of the swaying trees in his ears. He took a deep breath, and then he heard—or more, felt—something . . . someone behind him.

Lionel spun around, and there, standing not two paces away, was their grandfather.

Chapter Sixteen

Grandfather's Bow • News from the Outpost • Supplies

THAT NIGHT the children feasted on fresh venison from the large buck that Grandpa said Beatrice's missed shot had scared right toward him. The children did not hear their grandfather because he did not use a rifle to bring down the animal. Instead, he used a traditional bow and arrow that he had made based on what Napi the Old Man had taught the Blackfeet a long time ago.

"It might just be my opinion," their grandfather said as he turned the roasting meat, "but taking that buck's life with a bow is more honorable than with a rifle. It shows a mutual respect 'cuz it's more difficult. Gives them deers a fighting chance."

He cut a piece and handed it to Lionel with a

wink. "I'll leave the rest of this with you, Beatrice. Least I could do, seeing you sent the deer my way."

They ate the roasted venison and finished the last of the preserved stewed tomatoes that he had sent with Lionel and Beatrice when they had left his cabin on the river what now seemed like a lifetime ago. While they ate, their grandfather told them of his trip to the Boss Ribs' and then to the outpost.

Grandpa had left his cabin shortly after they had and wandered with Corn Poe in a roundabout way back to the Boss Ribs' place. He said that Corn Poe got a beating from his father for leaving, but Grandpa thought it was more for the work that didn't get done around the place as opposed to the family truly missing the boy.

Lionel felt bad for Corn Poe, but Grandpa said that he was fine and a good boy, aside from talking a bit too much. From the Boss Ribs', Grandpa rode his mule to the outpost to get news from the boarding school about the children's and Ulysses's disappearance.

The soldiers had questioned him when he arrived, and Grandpa told them that he had not known that the children were missing and was only at the school to visit them. The soldiers thought that this was a strange coincidence, but he acted as though he was mad at the priest, Brother Finn, and the captain for losing his only living kin. Grandpa told Lionel and Beatrice that he did not like to lie and prided himself that he hadn't done so since he was a kid, but that under the circumstances he did not see that there was another option, and that there was something about it that he had rather enjoyed.

The government sent out several parties to try to recover the horse, Lionel, and Beatrice, but due to the rough weather, and against the persistent argument of Sergeant Jenkins, they had turned back. There was a disagreement among the military men as to whether the children, let alone the horse, had even survived the initial storms. They also doubted if a boy, let alone a little girl, could make it through the late-winter snow and up into the mountains. Unfortunately, they planned to resume the search after the thaw.

Grandpa also heard that after a visit out to the Boss Ribs' place, and thanks to Corn Poe's big mouth, the soldiers were under the impression that the children had taken the horse to Canada. Lionel thought that Grandpa had begun to like Corn Poe's more mischievous side. He also thought that something about his grandfather seemed different. He seemed to be happier, and he now wore a second hawk's feather in his hair.

The three cleaned up from their supper and stoked the fire for the still-freezing night. Lionel washed the dishes with water carried up from the creek, while Beatrice and Grandpa unloaded the rest of the supplies from the travois behind the old mule. There were more canned preserves and vegetables, small burlap sacks of seeds for a garden, sacks of grain for Ulysses, more ammunition for the rifle, and a variety of other essentials such as flour, corn meal, matches, bar soap, and long tallow candles.

After washing the dishes, Lionel turned his attention toward Grandpa's bow and small quiver of handmade arrows. He marveled at the simple beauty of them, and before he knew it, found himself taking an arrow and placing it on the strung bow. Lionel heard Beatrice and Grandpa laughing as they came toward the door and thought that he might get in trouble for going through his grandfather's things. He spun around to replace the items, but as he did, he felt the arrow slip from the taut sinew string.

The arrow shot across the room just as Beatrice and Grandpa entered, then ricocheted off the stone fireplace.

"What in the hell?" Grandpa fell backward, knocking Beatrice to the floor and watching the arrow sail out the open door into the moonlight.

Lionel didn't know what to do, so he dropped the bow.

"I see you found the bow." Grandpa laughed as he slowly got back to his feet. "It's not bright to monkey with something that you know nothing about. That's how people get hurt."

Beatrice just stared at Lionel. Lionel felt like he was about two feet tall.

"Let's unpack the supplies and I'll tell ya all about it. Tomorrow I'll show you how to make your own bow and maybe, if you promise to hold your fire, teach you how to shoot."

They unpacked the supplies as Grandpa continued to tease Lionel about his archery skills. Lionel didn't mind, as it sure seemed to make Beatrice laugh. When Beatrice did laugh, which was not often, it was infectious. It started low, as a giggle, and slowly grew. She laughed herself into a coughing fit several times over the course of that evening.

Once the supplies were unpacked and their chores were done, the children settled in before the fire and their grandfather, sitting with his pipe in one of the old creaking chairs. They sat in silence for a while as Grandpa asked them to think about the day and to be happy for what they had. Lionel fell asleep lying next to his sister, appreciating the warmth of the buffalo robe. He did not remember having any dreams when he woke up the next morning.

Chapter Seventeen

An Ordered Lodge • Smoking Game • Old Man and the Buffalo • The Garden • Straw Man

The following day was busy and reminded Lionel of the hectic times back at the boarding school. They got up early and ate a breakfast of cold venison, canned peaches, and coffee. Then Grandpa led them to one of the small outbuildings that stood in shambles within the woods that surrounded the meadow and fallen lodge.

They cleared away the dense undergrowth, revealing the small encampment's smokehouse. Grandpa informed them that they must treat the game they killed if they wanted to preserve it and avoid getting sick.

Grandpa knocked out a small hole in the side of

the building with an ax and converted two old bean cans to replace the little building's rusted stovepipe. He placed the cans into the hole to keep a flow of air to the fire that they were going to build to smoke the meat.

Grandpa started the fire in their latest addition and asked Lionel to gather wood and stack it against the log sides. Then Grandpa and Beatrice cut the rest of the venison into strips, laid it out in the sun, and covered it with salt. Grandpa said that the salt would help to pull the moisture from the meat and prevent it from spoiling. They hung the salted strips in the smoky room; then Grandpa showed them how to clean the rest of the deer, carefully preserving each and every part.

"We'll make all kinds of tools for ya with the bones, and I'll bet we can fashion some sort of a shirt, maybe some leggings, from the hide."

"How about arrows? When are we going to make the arrows?" Lionel asked.

"Don't you even think about that until we get these chores done," Grandpa replied, turning his attention to the main lodge. He determined that although the roof seemed structurally sound, despite its sloping state, it wouldn't hurt to reinforce the sagging support beams.

They went into the woods, and Grandpa selected two tall, straight pine trees with Y-shaped branches near their tops to serve as the new supports. Grandpa thanked the pines for their service and then carefully cut the trees so that they fell where Grandpa instructed them. Lionel told Grandpa how he had led Ulysses directly into the lodge when Beatrice was tired after their long journey, and Grandpa thought that it was such a good idea that they should do the same with newly fallen timber. Grandpa also pointed out that by taking this course of action, they were in no way comparing Beatrice to the fallen logs.

They tied the trees to Grandpa's mule and dragged them right into the big main room. Then Grandpa tied a length of rope toward the top of one of the logs and threw the other end over the lodge's main support beam. He tied the loose end of the rope to the mule, and in no time they hoisted the log up and secured the V-shaped end into place as an additional brace. Ulysses watched them through the window from the meadow and seemed to approve of the process and the mule's work. They did the same with the second log, and when they had finished, Grandpa said that he would sleep easier that night.

Then, they cleaned the lodge. This really reminded Lionel of being back at school. Grandpa said that there was no way that the children could keep their heads straight if their lodge wasn't in order, so he sent Beatrice out to find a pine bough and showed her how to fasten the branches and some long dried grass to replace the broken broom. He then sent Lionel down to the stream with an old rusted bucket, and when he returned, put him to the task of cleaning and scrubbing every square inch of the lodge with an old bristle brush that they found in the small open-sided stable.

After the windows were washed and the lodge's floor scrubbed, they cleaned out the stable and assessed it for supplies. Over the next few days, they built a new outhouse from lumber that they found lying across the rafters of the stable, and they patched the sunken roof and collapsed side of the lodge as best they could. They salvaged what remained of the rat-ravaged grain stores and organized an array of rusting tools and farm implements.

Lionel looked around at their little lodge and

the outbuildings. He could not believe how much they had accomplished in the short time since their grandfather had arrived. "Looks pretty darn good, don't it?" Grandpa said, almost as if he was reading Lionel's mind. "But I'm wondering if you could do one more thing for me."

Lionel nodded and followed as his grandfather led him down to the stream.

"Remember me tellin' you how Napi created the land for the animals?"

"Yes, sir, of course."

"Then he created the people, right? Our people."

"Yes, sir."

"This here's the serviceberry," Grandpa said, reaching out to a spindly clump of bushes that grew near the stream. "Napi told the first people, the ones with the stone knives, to use this to make their arrows."

Lionel's face lit up in anticipation.

"Listen to me, Lionel. I want you to pick only the straightest branches you can find."

Lionel thought he was going to burst. He found several options and showed them to Grandpa, who carefully selected an assortment of the branches and boughs and brought them back to the front steps of the lodge.

Grandpa pulled a stool out into the late afternoon sun and sat down with his pocketknife in hand. "But did you ever wonder how the people knew what it was they should eat?"

Beatrice stepped out from the late afternoon darkness of the lodge.

"Well," Grandpa began, "Old Man gathered the people and showed them the buffalo. 'You must go down to the Great Plains and hunt them,' Napi told them. The people did, but the buffalo killed and ate them."

"Ate them?" Lionel interrupted. "Buffalo don't eat people."

Grandpa skinned the thin bark from the slender branches with his knife and continued, ignoring Lionel's question.

"Now, Old Man, he's a traveler, always on the move, so one day he came across the dead hunting party and felt bad. Old Man decided that the buffalo should not eat man, but that man should kill and eat the buffalo.

"The Old Man went out and found some of his

people who were still alive. 'I don't understand. I created the buffalo for you to eat. Why do you let them kill and eat you?'

"One of Old Man's children stepped forward. 'We don't have any weapons, and the buffalo does. He has horns to cut us down and is very fast and powerful.'

"Napi thought about it and realized that he must give the people something to even the odds against the buffalo."

"Like you and the deer," Lionel interrupted.

"So Old Man went out and searched the land," Grandpa continued, winking at Lionel. "Down by the river he found and cut some long thin branches of this here serviceberry bush."

Grandpa held the branch out for emphasis.

"Napi took the longest, widest, strongest branches he could find, stripped back the bark, and strung a strong piece of sinew to the end. He bent the branch and tied the sinew string to the other end to create the bow."

Lionel thought of his first encounter with Grandpa's bow, hoping that his next attempt would prove to be a greater success.

"The Old Man then took the thinner branches

and placed them on the string. He pulled the string tight and saw that although the smaller branch flew, it did not fly with any accuracy. The Old Man looked to the air and saw the birds and how they flew, dove, and darted. He called to the birds, and the birds gave him feathers from their wings. The Old Man tied the feathers to the end of the branch and again placed it onto the bow. This time the branch flew with greater accuracy but wouldn't stick when it hit its target. The Old Man decided to tie some of the hard stones from his pocket to the wood. He did this and once again put the branch with the feathers and stone to the bow. He pulled back on the string, and the branch flew, hitting its target with great accuracy and result. The feathers gave direction, the stones power.

"The Old Man turned to the people and said, 'This is the arrow. You should put it on the bow and go to hunt the buffalo.'

"The people went out to look for the buffalo and found 'em. The buffalo also saw the people and thought, Here is our food, we should go and eat them. But this time the people did not run, and when the buffalo circled around them, they took the arrow and the bow and shot the buffalo.

"You know, they say that when the first buffalo was hit, he cried out, 'A fly bit me.' Then just fell over dead," Grandpa said as he stripped the last small branch of its bark. "You two should scour the woods for some feathers from our flying friends."

Lionel and Beatrice did as they were told, and although the feathers were more difficult to locate when one was actually looking for them, they returned with an assortment of discarded tail and wing feathers from a turkey, raven, and even a blue jay. Grandpa split the quills of the feathers with his folding knife and carefully tied them to the ends of the slender sticks.

"I think we can hold off on the arrowheads until you get a better idea of how this all works," Grandpa said as he attached a sinew string that he had made from the deer that now hung in the smokehouse.

They spent the rest of the day, and in Lionel's case into the early evening, practicing with their new bows and arrows. That night they roasted venison over the fire, and Grandpa sat smoking his pipe and carving an assortment of arrowheads from the bones of the deer.

The next day, the bows and arrows were set aside

as Grandpa taught Lionel and Beatrice how to dig a garden. There was a rusted shovel, a hoe, and a pick from the stable; and with Grandpa standing over them, the children soon turned a sunny patch of the meadow into a good-sized rectangle of rich, black soil. They selected an area close to the stream for hauling water, and then Grandpa sent them into the woods to gather dried leaves and moss that he spread and mixed into the freshly turned soil. As they dug, their grandfather was busy lashing and then weaving an odd assortment of grass and tree limbs.

"What is that?" Lionel asked, eager to take a late-morning break from the heavy digging.

"You'll see" was all that Grandfather said. "You'll see."

After they had turned the soil to Grandpa's satisfaction, he sent Lionel into the lodge for the sacks of seeds that he had brought on his old mule.

"We've got tomatoes, corn, carrots, turnips, sunflowers, squash, pole beans, and maybe even some watermelon," Grandpa said as he showed the children how to plant the precious seeds in their carefully built up rows. "You're going to have pay close attention to these crops: they're your life now."

Once the seeds were planted, Grandpa sent them for rusty bucket after rusty bucket of water.

"Plenty of water, plenty of water," Grandpa repeated as he continued to weave the grass, leaves, and tree branches together with his thick hands.

The suspense was killing Lionel. "What is it?" he pleaded.

"Why, don't you see?" Grandpa said, rising from the old creaking stool that still sat in the yard. "It's the straw man, who's going to protect all your hard work."

Sure enough, standing almost as tall as Grandpa, there was his creation. The straw man's lifelike arms, legs, and chest were a tight weave of serviceberry boughs and tall grass that grew on the banks of the stream. His head was the leaf-stuffed old grain sack that Ulysses was pulling when Lionel awoke that first day in the meadow.

Grandpa fastened three turkey feathers to the straw man's head and hung him on a tall lodge pole toward the far end of the garden facing the river.

"I think he'll do a fine job, but this is a team. Don't you leave it just to him now, you hear? No, sir, you'll have to watch for yerselves too, especially for them old rabbits or squirrels. Squirrels love corn. So, watch 'em!"

That afternoon, they continued to practice with the bow and arrows, and that night they found themselves once again in front of the fire with Grandpa telling them stories from when their people ruled the Great Plains.

"The soldiers never did make us leave, ya know," Grandpa said between long draws from his pipe. "I'm pretty sure we're the only tribe whose reservation is on our own hunting grounds, not where the government told us to go. We stayed where we were, and although our land is a bit smaller, we're still here."

Chapter Eighteen

Lionel's Nightmare • Bear Claws •
Grandpa's Candor • Grizzly

Early the next morning, when it was still dark, Lionel woke up covered in sweat with Grandpa standing over him.

"You're having a dream, Lionel. Take a deep breath. It will be all right."

Lionel sat up and looked around. He was in the little lodge in the meadow by the stream. Beatrice slept soundly next to him; Grandpa crouched beside them, eerily lit by the low firelight.

"You all right?" Grandpa whispered.

Lionel nodded. Grandpa stood up, and in two long, silent strides, was at the door. Lionel wasn't sure if you could inherit the ability to move the way that Grandpa and Beatrice did, but he thought that they both, when they wanted to, moved in similar fashion.

Lionel got up and threw on his clothes to follow, and soon the two were halfway across the moonlit meadow heading toward the stream.

"Don't want to wake up Beatrice. I figure we might get some morning air."

Lionel looked up at the sky. It was still dark, the stars dancing overhead. They walked in silence. Lionel thought about his dream. He had been back on the shore of the river, but the river had grown into a sea of rolling grass. Grandpa and Beatrice, even Corn Poe, were gone. Lionel was left alone, or so he thought. Lionel turned from the water and saw the Frozen Man. Although he still appeared to be frozen, the man was walking. Walking toward Lionel.

Lionel did not know what to do, so he held his ground. Although he was scared, he told himself that he had nothing to fear. He had never harmed the Frozen Man in any way, unless the man was upset that he'd taken the bear claws. Lionel took a step back, but then he noticed that the man held out his arm, and that in his hand was the bear claw necklace, as though he was offering it to Lionel.

Lionel felt bad for the man and thought about giving him his jacket, or that he should make a fire to help warm him, but his gestures were interrupted by the thunderous approach of a horse's hooves. Lionel turned to find Sergeant Jenkins riding wildly toward them.

Sergeant Jenkins rode fast on a horse as black as midnight. Lionel did not know why, but in his dream he stepped in front of the Frozen Man to try to protect him. What was he, a little boy, going to do?

That was when Lionel woke up, and now he was walking with Grandpa across the meadow wet with early-morning dew. The image of Jenkins's scar-snarled face and the lonely icy pale look of the Frozen Man sent a chill up Lionel's spine.

"You cold?" Grandpa asked.

"No, just thinking about my dream."

"They're powerful, ya know. Dreams. You should pay attention to them like ya pay attention to all that's around you. The trees, the mountain, the birds, this stream, like I said, it's all talking to you."

They walked up to the water's edge, and Grandpa sat on a boulder. Lionel looked upstream. The water came down heavy with snowmelt from above them. It crashed, cascading in a spiral of waterfalls over giant boulders of granite.

Lionel sat on a small rock next to Grandpa and started to cry. He didn't know why he was crying but could no longer control it. Grandpa didn't say anything. He just put his arm around the boy, and they sat surrounded by darkness until the first hint of morning crept into the eastern sky.

"Grandpa?" Lionel asked. "I think I have something I want to show you. I didn't show it to no one, not even Beatrice."

"That's up to you, Lionel."

Lionel took the bear claws from the pocket of his coat and held them out, as the Frozen Man seemed to have held them out to Lionel.

"This belonged to the Frozen Man back at the school that Beatrice told you about."

Lionel's grandfather took the heavy necklace and ran the thick bear claws through his fingers. He turned each claw over, studying the meticulous beading. He twisted the smooth buffalo leather that connected them and felt the shiny claw tips, as if he were testing their readiness.

"Ulysses took me to him back at the school.

When I found him he was holding these out . . . that's how it looked to me. I took them right before the soldiers got there. They took everything else."

"This is special, Lionel, and I think it is better that you have it instead of them government men." As Grandpa handed back the necklace, he looked over to the stable where Ulysses stood with his mule. "Maybe the man tried to give it to the horse, and the horse wanted you to have it or to hold it for him?"

Lionel thought about it. That was possible. He and Ulysses had been friends since the first day they'd met. Lionel's mind was racing again.

"But, Grandpa, I still don't understand—where did the Frozen Man go?"

"To be honest with you, Lionel, I don't know. And despite what they all say, no one knows."

"They don't?"

"No, they sure don't. How could they?" Grandpa said as he pulled out his pipe and tobacco pouch.

He stood and pulled some of the stringy leaves and raised them toward the rising sun, then let the tobacco drift from his fingers, carried away by the slight breeze that rose from the stream. He turned and offered his tobacco to the south, west, and north, like Beatrice had back at the school. He then sat down on the rock, loaded his pipe, and smoked.

"I'm sorry you had to see this side of our people and of the government. I'm confused as to how we let it get like this. I think that we should sit here and think about what has happened."

And so they sat on the bank of the stream, watching the sun break through the early-morning clouds that hung over them and the mountains. Lionel did as he was told and thought about all that had happened since they had left the boarding school, and before. He thought about the captain and the priest, Barney Little Plume giving the candy to Delores Ground, and the sheep shears sticking out of Sergeant Jenkins's hand.

Lionel could still see Big Bull Boss Ribs and then the look on Corn Poe's face when they first saw Grandpa and thought that he was a ghost or a spirit. He thought about Beatrice and how she silently did what she thought or knew she had to do, and how she had kept him warm despite the freezing cold that they encountered on their long ride into the mountains. He pictured his grandfather and how much wilder he looked when he rejoined them in the Great Wood.

Then Lionel thought about the broken string of bear claws and the Frozen Man.

"Lionel," his grandfather said in a low whisper, "do you smell that?"

"Smell what?" Lionel asked.

Lionel's grandfather responded by taking a deep breath. Lionel did the same. At first, he took in what he had become accustomed to—the smell of the smoke from their fire, wet grass, the high pine, and the familiar smell of Ulysses and Grandpa's mule—but then, he sensed something different. It reminded Lionel of the steam that had risen from Ulysses's back as Beatrice pushed the horse up the frozen river before they entered the mountains. But this smell was wilder.

Grandpa raised a single finger to his lips and slowly turned upstream. Lionel's eyes followed, and there, not two hundred paces away, was a grizzly bear.

The bear was situated in one of a series of pools, his giant paws clawing at the water that tumbled around him. Lionel looked to his grandfather, who sat calmly on his boulder smoking his pipe as if they were watching the Fourth of July horse races down at the soldiers' fort.

Lionel looked at the grizzly and thought about the necklace that hung in his grandfather's hand. What if the bear saw the claws and became angry? What if the claws were from a friend or family member? Or, Lionel thought, the claws could also be from one of the bear's enemies, and perhaps they could be friends because the Frozen Man had killed the bear's enemy for him. Lionel hoped that this was true, and that the bear would consider them to be his friends.

The grizzly continued to swat at the swell, occasionally submerging his entire head beneath the pool's surface until one giant swoop from his great paw sent a silver flash up and onto the riverbank. The grizzly turned, looked directly at Lionel and his grandfather, and then rumbled slowly upstream with a giant fish held securely in its mouth.

Lionel couldn't believe what he'd seen. His body tingled with excitement, and his first thought was to run back to the lodge to tell Beatrice. But that wasn't necessary. Beatrice was standing behind him.

"I hope you two took note of your new neighbor," Grandpa told them.

Beatrice smiled and headed back to the lodge. Lionel sat on his rock. He still could not believe that they had seen the bear.

"I think we can take that to mean that you have their blessings," Grandpa said as he took the string of bear claws and tied them around Lionel's neck. He stood and followed Beatrice back to the lodge.

Lionel sat, feeling the heavy weight of the bear claws, and thinking about all that his grandfather had said.

Chapter Nineteen

The Straw Man in Silk • Chores • Bear Cave • Roots • The Old Man and the Berries

When Lionel crossed the meadow, he noticed that the straw man perched over the garden had changed. He no longer wore the old pants and shirt that Grandpa had originally dressed him in. He now stood watch in the torn ivory silk dress that Beatrice had abandoned.

Lionel returned to the lodge to find a breakfast of smoked venison and canned peaches waiting for him. They ate, and then Grandpa put the children back to work. They gathered firewood, watered the garden, and repaired various neglected items found around the lodge.

Later that day they returned to the stream and

followed the bear's tracks to a small cave about two and a half miles from their meadow. Grandpa felt that it was wise to let the bear be, but wanted the children to know where he was in relation to their new home. Grandpa was confident that as long as Lionel and Beatrice were aware and respectful, they would get along just fine with their neighbor.

They made their way back to the meadow, their grandfather stopping along the way to show them the various roots and berries that were edible and the plants that were not. When they arrived at the stream, their grandfather stopped at a large huckleberry bush with long branches that hung over the bank.

"Did I tell you about the Old Man and the berries?" he asked, removing his coat.

"No, you didn't," Beatrice answered as Grandpa spread his coat beneath the largest of the berry bushes.

"Lionel, hand me the stick over there."

Lionel picked up a large stick and handed it to their grandfather.

"One day Old Man was out doin' his travelin' and he came to a stream, well, kinda like this one. Old Man was thirsty, so he lay down on the bank to drink, but, to his surprise, noticed that there were berries all over the rocky bottom."

Lionel looked into the swilling waters that rushed past them. Unlike in the clear pool where the bear had been fishing, you could not see the bottom; so Lionel did not see any berries.

"The Old Man was hungry so he dove into the water to collect the berries. He swam around, diving to the bottom repeatedly, but couldn't find them. As you might imagine, the Old Man got tired and pulled himself back onto the bank and collapsed under the shade of the bushes that grew alongside the stream. He slept in the shade for most of that afternoon, but when he woke, he was looking up into the bush above him. There the Old Man saw the berries and realized that their reflection in the water had tricked him."

"He thought that the berries grew under the water?" Lionel said with a giggle.

"He sure did and felt mighty stupid for doin' so. He got so mad that he picked up a stick, like this one I got right here," Grandpa said, raising the small club over his head, "and beat the bushes, I mean he really gave 'em a thrashing."

Grandpa brought the stick down hard, whacking the shrub mercilessly.

"Well, what do you think happened?" Grandpa continued as he raised the stick again and again. "All of them berries fell to the ground, giving the Old Man another lesson to teach his people."

Lionel watched the berries fall to Grandpa's coat.

"So, who wants to eat some berries?" Grandfather concluded, throwing a handful into his mouth, then adding, "Close, but not quite ripe."

That night the children once again gathered around the fire. Lionel didn't feel well, because once he started to eat the berries, ripe or not, he couldn't stop and soon ate himself into a stomachache. After several trips to the outhouse, his belly felt better, but he still lay flat on his back in front of the fire, occasionally sitting up to drink some cool water from the stream out of his tin cup.

Grandpa and Beatrice worked the hide from another deer that Grandpa had shot. He had instructed her to chew on it and to work it in her hands to make it soft and easier to cut into the leggings and shirt that he planned to make for them.

Grandpa also cut strips of leather and set them aside, letting Lionel know that these were for him when his hair had grown long enough to warrant them.

Lionel thought that this was the happiest time that he could ever remember. He figured that Beatrice must have agreed, because although she still kept to herself and did not speak much, she was always happy, a smile stretched across her face. Lionel hated to think of having to go back to the school and its dreary, worn-down classrooms. The thought of the school's gray, tasteless stew compared with what he had eaten since they had arrived at the lodge was enough in itself. He hoped that they never had to leave.

CHAPTER TWENTY

BUCKSKINS • WORDS OF ADVICE • FAREWELL

THE NEXT morning, their grandfather woke them and told them to dress. Lionel crawled from beneath the buffalo robe and stumbled to his clothes, which were stacked in a neat pile next to the fireplace. Folded on top, Lionel found the buckskin leggings. He looked over excitedly and saw Beatrice pulling on her new shirt.

Along with her long braids and hawk feathers, Beatrice looked like a page from the painted picture book of "savages" that the Brothers had showed Lionel once in the library at the boarding school. Well, except for the fact the painted "savage" in the book wore a fierce scowl, not the ear-to-ear grin that was plastered across Beatrice's beaming face.

Once dressed, they had berries and coffee for breakfast—Lionel showing better judgment this time as to the amount of berries he ate. Then their grandfather walked them through all that he had showed them, starting at the stream with the berries, then turning to the garden, the Great Wood, and the smokehouse.

They returned to the lodge, and Grandpa brought his mule around and loaded up his gear. While he packed, Beatrice and Lionel sat with him; Beatrice doing her best to tie small cardinal and blue jay feathers into Lionel's growing hair.

Then Grandpa cinched the last of his belongings. "Well, I best be goin'. The soldiers will be back by my place the day after next. I counted."

He kneeled down and pulled Lionel and Beatrice close.

"They make their rounds about every ten days or so, and I'm sure they'll be eager to come by my place and check for you. Soldiers are prone to stick to their habits, I've noticed."

Grandpa looked sad as he hugged them. He stood and threw his leg over his old mule.

"You two take care of each other, you hear? I'll

be back as soon as I can, and we'll figure out our next move." Then he spun his mule around and vanished into the Great Wood.

A dark sense of melancholy hung over Lionel and Beatrice that afternoon. They stayed busy, continuing their grandfather's prescribed daily regimen of tending the garden and practicing with their bows and arrows, but it wasn't the same.

As the days passed, their moods improved, and they soon found themselves laughing and taking turns telling each other of the travels of Napi the Old Man and counting down the days until their grandfather's return.

Chapter Twenty-One

Long Days, Cool Nights • Drums in the Deep Woods • Bushwhacked

Spring soon turned to summer, and the children did as their grandfather had taught them. They swam in the cool pools of the stream and raided the hillsides for blackberries and raspberries, much like the grizzly. They dug for grubs and beetles under the rotted logs of the forest as they had observed the wolverine and the badger do. Like the hawk and eagle, they waited patiently for the precise moment before releasing the taut string of the bow while hunting the squirrels and rabbits; and they silently stalked the elk and deer just like the mountain lion.

Their feet grew tough; Lionel's hair grew long; and Beatrice's grew longer. In their buckskin leggings and shirts that Grandpa had made, it would have been hard for anyone from the boarding school to even recognize them.

They started each day by swimming in the stream. Then they saw to the garden or hunted or fished, depending on what the stores in the smokehouse dictated. At night they sat around the fire making arrows or lay in the cool grass of the meadow, staring up at the endless sea of stars.

The children cut the hides and skins of the elk and deer from their hunts and fashioned them into clothes to repair or replace the worn-out wool and heavy canvas garments that had been issued back on the reservation. They missed their grandfather but soon came to enjoy the solace of their new home and made friends with their neighbors the grizzly, raven, wolverine, and the other creatures that occupied the Great Wood.

After a while, Lionel noticed that Beatrice was growing anxious that their grandfather still had not returned. She checked the food stores and then decided that they should venture deeper into the Great Wood to hunt, and to see if the thaw had brought any signs of trouble from the government men or the school.

That night they cleaned the rifle and packed a

bushel of berries and what remained of the smoked meat. They fastened quivers made of birchbark and filled them with the arrows that their grandfather had showed them how to make. Beatrice collected feathers from the edge of the Great Wood and wove them into Ulysses's long, flowing mane, and when they woke early the next morning they were prepared for their latest excursion.

The children rode out of the meadow high on Ulysses's back, looking every bit the young wanted warrior outlaws that they now were. They rode through the Great Wood and continued up into a strange tangle of trees that they had never seen before. Game was surprisingly scarce, and Lionel began to wonder who or what had scared it all away.

By midday the woods opened, and Lionel questioned how far they planned to travel from the lodge in the meadow. Sometime that afternoon they heard what they thought to be the distant sounds of drums. Beatrice proceeded toward the drums with caution, and soon the woods once again grew thick and the trees began to twist and turn their branches, tying themselves in knots overhead. Then the drumming stopped.

For some reason this scared Lionel more than the sound of them beating. Beatrice pulled Ulysses up and listened.

"What is it?" Lionel whispered.

"I'm not sure," Beatrice answered. "Something ain't right."

The next thing Lionel knew, he was knocked from Ulysses's back and had landed with a thud on the thick carpet of the forest floor. He rolled over as soon as he hit the ground and saw Beatrice lying next to him with a large, fat boy standing over her.

Beatrice tried to get to her feet, but the boy knocked Beatrice back to the ground and then stood over her, clucking and pawing at the dirt like an overstuffed prairie chicken. The boy had feathers in his hair, and he began to squawk and occasionally jumped sideways, striking Beatrice with the end of a short stick as he did.

Lionel looked around and saw that the boy was not alone. The trees seemed to come alive with children, ranging from Lionel's age to well over Beatrice's.

The other children—Lionel counted ten—circled them. One by one they stepped forward, trying to grab ahold of Ulysses's rawhide reins. Beatrice sprang to her feet, driving the fat boy back and knocking a smaller kid away from Ulysses's right flank.

Lionel grabbed the reins from Beatrice and backed himself and Ulysses against the trunk of a large tree. Beatrice turned to face the fat boy. He stomped at the ground and continued to shriek and jump from side to side. Beatrice circled him patiently, and the next time he lunged at her, she twisted him sideways and threw him over her leg. The boy hit the ground hard, and in a flash Beatrice had Grandpa's knife nestled between the folds of his chubby throat.

She looked up at Lionel, who along with Ulysses held off the other boys. "That's enough," Beatrice announced.

The children stopped and turned to her. Her braids with their hawk feathers fell to the sides of her face, the knife catching the slightest hint of the late afternoon sun through the trees.

"He won't do it," cried the fat one, mistaking Beatrice for a boy. "Get the horse!"

The rest of the children, Lionel included, froze, unsure of what to do. Lionel looked around at the faces of their attackers. They were painted, some of them poorly, and they wore an odd combination of government-issued uniforms and makeshift versions of the traditional clothing of the Blackfeet.

Lionel recognized the school uniforms from the day of the football game. They were from the Heart Butte boarding school, and the fat boy was Barney Little Plume.

"Get off of me," Barney screamed, wrestling Beatrice with little success. Beatrice held him firmly to the ground, the knife carefully hovering over his throat. "I was just counting coo. Get the hell off!"

Ulysses was doing a good job of keeping the rest of the children back, but Lionel was having trouble hanging on to the reins, the big horse pulling him from the tree and dragging him sideways with his sporadic leaping kicks. Lionel wrapped the leather strap around his hand and held the horse as best he could. Ulysses jumped again, and Lionel lost his footing but somehow managed to hold on.

"Come on now, easy, boy. Calm down, you're gonna be all right."

Lionel looked up and saw a boy slowly moving toward Ulysses, his voice just a notch above a whisper.

"Remember me? Sure ya do. You're gonna be all right. There's nothin' for a big old horse like you to be scared of. . . ."

It was Corn Poe, Corn Poe Boss Ribs. Lionel wasn't sure who was more surprised to see the boy—Beatrice, Ulysses, or himself, but he noticed that Corn Poe's soothing voice was having an effect on the horse.

Lionel tucked the bear claws into his shirt and got to his feet to help Corn Poe bring the big horse around. Corn Poe looked different. His skin was tan with summer, and his hair had indeed grown out. True to his promise, tattered feathers and tiny strips of flannel were knotted in his hair; his clothes were dirty and torn to shreds.

"Corn Poe?" Beatrice said, with her knife still at Barney's throat.

"You know them?" Barney responded, having given up his struggle.

"Sure," said Corn Poe. "That there's Lionel and this is Beatrice."

"Beatrice?" Barney stammered, looking at her clearly for the first time. "You're a girl? But you're the same sonuvagun that broke my leg."

Chapter Twenty-Two

Renegades • Corn Poe's Metamorphosis • Old Man Steals from the Sun

Beatrice eventually let Barney up and Corn Poe did his best to calm things, introducing his two friends to this newly formed band of renegades. The children walked back to their camp as Corn Poe told them of news from the outpost and how he came to be in the woods with Barney and the other Heart Butte students. Beatrice helped two of the smaller children onto Ulysses's back and then led the horse by the reins. Barney walked at their side.

After the soldiers questioned Corn Poe in the Boss Ribs' valley, he took another beating from his father and decided that enough was enough. He stole one of his father's horses with the intention of joining

Beatrice and Lionel in the mountains. That was over two weeks ago, and now the horse was dead.

Corn Poe ate what he could of the horse, but besides that, he'd had little in the way of food. He survived the journey to the edge of the woods by raiding the small gardens and chicken coops that he found along the way. He wandered in the Great Wood for three days before he found this band from Heart Butte.

"There weren't much news from the fort, exceptin' that they started to send out search parties again and that the one that calls himself Jenkins claims he's gonna kill you," Corn Poe concluded, pointing at Beatrice.

Barney punctuated this grim announcement by staring at Beatrice. Beatrice seemed to be unaffected, but the whole exchange weighed heavily on Lionel's mind.

Lionel walked along among this ragtag group, eventually wondering out loud, "How did the rest of you end up out here?"

"They wouldn't let us from the Heart Butte School go to the Fourth of July horse races and Pow-Wow. They think that we're makin' good progress at not bein' heathen and didn't want us to get wrongly influenced by the old folks, so we run away and come out here on our own accord."

They continued walking until the thick canopy overhead began to thin. There, the wood opened into a clearing, and in the midst of it stood a small hovel covered in army blankets and animal skins. There was also the remnant of a large fire. A cold-water creek ran through the far side of the trees.

"We're having our own Pow-Wow," Barney went on. "I know we'll catch hell when we get back, but it's worth it. I'm tired of them telling us what we can and can't do."

They entered the small camp, and a couple of children set about gathering more wood and starting the fire. Barney sat down on the ground and someone brought him a bucket of water from the creek. He drank from it and then offered it to Beatrice.

"What about you? I heard y'all ran away and stole the captain's horse. Where you been keeping yerselves?"

"Just travelin' the woods," Beatrice said. "Headin' north."

"Yeah, that's what I heard. To Canada."

"Ycp, Canada."

"Ya know the government put a bounty on yer heads? Five bucks a piece for your return, fifty for the horse."

Beatrice looked up at Barney with an icy stare. "Is that right?"

"Yep, and they're offerin' up to ten whole cents for a gopher tail," Corn Poe spat. "Tryin' to rid the reservation of 'em for the farmers."

Lionel looked over at Corn Poe, who stood over the fire. He couldn't believe how different he looked. He thought that he must have grown a couple of inches to boot.

Corn Poe threw some more wood on the fire. "We're gonna do a sweat, then dance. Last night I had a vision."

"You ever had the vision?" Barney said, standing.

Beatrice shook her head.

"You should stay and join us," Barney replied, placing a couple of smooth river stones directly into the hot coals. "We'll heat these up and then bring 'em into the lodge. Pour on some water and they steam 'er right up.

"Saaám," Barney concluded, more to Beatrice than anyone else.

Beatrice nodded as if she understood.

"We ain't ate nothing in two days. Barely had any water. Right, Barney?" Corn Poe added. "Helps you get your vision."

They sat by the fire, heating the rocks as the day crept across the woods into early evening. Lionel was hungry. He thought about the food that he and Beatrice had packed and was troubled that he would not be able to touch it until after the ceremony had taken place. Lionel considered that he and his sister had already done this ceremony "of not eating" the two days after they left the school, and he wasn't all that excited about doing it again, especially when, this time around, they had more of a choice in the matter.

Barney stepped around the fire and toward Ulysses. Ulysses pawed at the earth and lowered his ears.

"Didn't this horse win the pull last year?" Barney asked, trying to smooth Ulysses's mane.

"Might have," Beatrice answered suspiciously.

"Yeah, I can see why they put up the fifty. That there is a helluva horse you stole." Barney left Ulysses and sat back down by the fire. "Did you ever hear about Napi the Old Man?"

Lionel looked up, full of excitement. "Yeah, our grandpa told us about him."

"He used to *steal* things too," Barney said, poking a stick into the fire and looking at Beatrice.

Lionel noticed that Beatrice didn't like the way that Barney emphasized the word "steal."

"No, we never heard about that," Lionel said.

"You ever hear that Old Man and the Sun were friends?"

"The sun?" Lionel responded, now more confused than ever.

"You betcha, and they loved to hunt. See, the Old Man liked venison, so he says, 'I like venison. Let's go hunt some deers.' That's all it took. So, the twose of 'em got their kit together for the hunt, with the Sun bringing out the most beautiful pair of leggings that Napi the Old Man had ever seen. Porcupine quills were embroidered down the sides, along with feathers and pieces of strange shells the likes of which he'd never before laid eyes on."

Lionel noticed that Corn Poe was reaching across a small kid sitting next to him, trying to touch the leggings that Lionel's grandfather had made him. Beatrice saw too and promptly reached out and slapped Corn Poe's hand.

"'These here leggings carry big medicine,' the Sun told the Old Man. 'When I'm wearing them, all I have to do is walk around a bush and it will light on fire. The fire drives all of the deers out of hiding so that we can hunt them.'

"With that, the two went out to hunt, and just as the Sun had said, the first bush they passed burst into flames. Two large white-tailed bucks ran from the brush, and the Sun and the Old Man shot them. That night they went back to the Sun's lodge, ate well, and with bellies full of venison, turned in. . . .

"But the Old Man could not sleep. He knew that the Sun was his friend, but he could not help but think about stealing the leggings from him.

"With them leggings, I'd never go hungry, the Old Man thought. So, that night, after everyone was sound asleep, he stole them."

With this, Barney looked from Beatrice to Ulysses. Beatrice looked from Barney to her knife.

"Old Man ran as fast and as far as he could," Barney continued. "But after a while he got tired, so he lay down, resting his head on the leggings, and fell asleep. The next morning the Old Man woke and sat up with a start. He was back in the Sun's lodge.

"'Old Man,' the Sun asked, 'why are my leggings under your head?'

"The Old Man looked around. He couldn't understand how he was back in the Sun's lodge.

"'Old Man, did you not hear me? Why are my leggings under your head?'

"'Oh,' the Old Man said, 'I couldn't find anything else for a pillow.'"

"A pillow?" Corn Poe blurted out. "Did they even have pillows back then?"

Barney answered by reaching over and popping Corn Poe on the back of the head. "That's how I heard it. You mind if I finish?"

"No, go right ahead. Just wonderin'," Corn Poe returned sheepishly.

"Well, the Sun believed him 'cuz they were friends, see? So, that night when they went to sleep, the Old Man stole them leggings again. This time, Old Man didn't stop running until almost morning. He was so tired he put the leggings under his head and again fell asleep. When the Old Man woke, he was once again in the Sun's Lodge. Old Man realized that the whole world is the Sun's lodge and that the Sun was on to him.

"The Sun stood over the Old Man and said, 'Pillow or not, seems that you like my leggings. If this is true, I will give them to you.' The Old Man said that it was true, thanked the Sun, and quickly went away.

"The Old Man continued his travels. He wandered across the land until he was out of food. Then he put on the leggings and set fire to the brush to hunt. Once again, the fire drove the deers toward him, but the Old Man noticed that the fire was getting close, so he ran away. But the fire chased him. Old Man ran faster, but the fire gained on him, and the leggings caught on fire. Old Man ran to the river. He jumped in, but when he hit the water, the burned leggings fell to pieces and floated down the river. Old Man couldn't handle them leggings."

"Boy, I'll say," Corn Poe emphasized.

"I think the Sun gave them leggings to the Old Man to teach him a lesson." Barney looked around dramatically. "You can't escape the Sun. He sees everything."

Barney sat silently for a moment and then motioned to one of the smaller children to bring the hot rocks into the sweat lodge. Barney drank what remained in the rusty bucket and tossed it toward another kid, who immediately picked it up and proceeded to the creek.

Lionel didn't like the way that Barney pushed the other children around. It reminded him of the constant orders and directions back at the boarding school.

"Sstsiiysskaan nin," Barney said, standing and stripping off his clothes down to his dirty long underwear. "I don't think that they usually allow the women. . . ."

But Beatrice did not let Barney finish. She stood, pushing past him toward the sweat lodge. She threw open the deer-hide flap, and looked inside.

"Kitái'kó'pohpa?" Barney pushed, calling into question Beatrice's bravery.

Beatrice answered by stripping off her clothes, pausing only as she undid her belt to look at the sheath knife that Grandpa had given her. Lionel watched as she carefully wrapped the knife in her bundle of clothes and then disappeared into the low structure.

Barney did the same, and when he did, two smaller children pulled hot rocks from the fire and followed.

"Let's go," Corn Poe said, stripping off his clothes and following. Lionel took another look at Ulysses, then at the setting sun, and followed the others.

Chapter Twenty-Three

The Sweat • A Vision • Black Mask • Bonfires & Corn Liquor • Eluding Barney Little Plume

Lionel ducked his head and crawled into the sweat lodge. It was smaller than he expected, and he immediately tripped over Corn Poe's feet and fell forward onto Beatrice and Barney. Barney roughly shoved him to his left, where Lionel had to immediately move to make room for another kid about Barney's age but as skinny as Barney was fat.

"I'm Tom," the skinny kid said. "Tom Gunn."

Tom sat in between Lionel and Corn Poe. "You're a helluva a ballplayer there, Beatrice. The Headmaster's gonna go red when he finds out you're a girl."

Tom had two sad-looking turkey quills, one of

them bent, hanging from his hair. They'd lost most of their down and feather somewhere long ago. "Good to meet you," he said, extending his hand. Beatrice shook it and then moved to the side for a kid who had entered with a bucket of cold water.

Toward the center of the lodge was a ring of stones, and in the middle of that there was already a pile of river rocks. The kid poured the water onto the rocks, and they immediately erupted in a cacophony of pops and sizzles, spitting hot, frothy bubbles onto Lionel's and the other children's feet.

Barney held a bundle of sweet grass before him, then lit it with a blue-tipped match. Smoke from the grass rose in translucent wisps toward the center of the lodge. Lionel watched as it climbed upward and then hung a few feet above their heads. He was already light-headed, hot and sitting so close to the other children, sweating. Barney was the worst, he thought. Rivers fell from the folds of his flesh, splashing onto Lionel with his every turn, nod, or jiggle—and one time he sneezed, showering all in an explosion of perspiration and mucus.

Barney sang a low song similar to the song that Beatrice had sung back at the chapel. He then held the grass under his face and passed the bundle to his left to Lionel. Lionel held the grass in front of him and took in the sweet, smoky smell. It reminded him of the rolling open prairie where the boarding school sat, and the summers they had spent working with the Brothers in the fields behind the school.

Lionel looked at Beatrice, who motioned gently with her eyes to his left. He passed the sweet grass on to Tom, who inhaled the smoke and then passed it to a small boy who now sat next to Corn Poe.

When it came to Corn Poe he took the grass and held it above his head. He started to sing a low song that didn't stay low for long. It grew quickly, and in Lionel's opinion was more reminiscent of the music that was played when the captain's wife had taught them the Virginia Reel and Lionel had danced with Delores Ground. He wondered if Delores remembered him or if she would even recognize him. He wondered what Corn Poe was praying for.

Lionel wasn't sure how long they sat there. He leaned his head back against the bent-bough skin of the structure and listened to Barney tell them of his exploits back at the Heart Butte school. Lionel figured he must have fallen asleep for a minute, because somehow Barney's explanation turned into Beatrice's story of the Old Man creating their world and showing them how to make the bow and arrow.

Lionel was hot and hungry. He wanted to drink some of the cool water that Barney periodically threw onto the hot rocks, but he did not want to leave. A strange feeling came over him, and he fell easily back into the stories that Barney and Beatrice told. He thought that he must have fallen asleep a second time, because he once again saw his grandfather and Beatrice on the raft in the sea of rolling grass. He still stood on the shore, but again wasn't alone. This time he was with a bear, the grizzly bear that he had seen with his grandfather the day that he had told him about the Frozen Man and the necklace. He felt the bear claws around his neck and wondered if the big bear was fishing. Lionel stood on the shore with the bear and knew that they were friends. Then he saw Corn Poe.

"I heard about it at the school. I went through what these learned men, like Barney over there, call a metamorphosis," Lionel woke up to hear Corn Poe saying. "The former me? Why, he's dead, dead, dead. Now I just gotta figure out this new one."

Barney handed Corn Poe a small wooden bowl. Corn Poe's fingers disappeared into the bowl, then reappeared covered in a paste of what appeared to be black ashes. He spread the concoction onto to his face and then passed the bowl to Barney, who did the same. Lionel wasn't sure what they were trying to do, and this was the first time that it occurred to him that neither Barney nor Corn Poe did, either. It seemed like they were making it up as they went along, but so far, he thought it was better than sitting back at school in the chapel.

"Now it's time to dance," Corn Poe said, attempting to rise. He stood up for a minute, teetered back and forth, and then stumbled to the ground, landing on top of the little kid. "Whoa, I guess I got me a tad bit of the light-headed."

Corn Poe crawled, mumbling, toward the opening, then threw the flap upward, filling the sweat lodge with crisp evening air. The coolness hit Lionel, driving the dizziness from his head. The little kid and then Tom followed Corn Poe, and soon Lionel did the same.

It was dark, and a thousand stars now littered the heavens. Lionel took a deep breath, then followed Corn Poe and the other children's voices as they cascaded through the darkness from somewhere down toward the creek.

Lionel reached the creek just as Corn Poe jumped from its muddy bank. He disappeared for a second under the swirling waters and then shot up and pulled himself to shore. Tom and the little kid followed, and then Lionel.

Lionel hit the near-freezing water and felt a jolt run through his body. He broke the surface and in a few short strokes was at the muddy bank. He drank from the cold creek, and then Corn Poe and Tom pulled him to his feet.

"I don't know what time it is, but I sure as hell know I'm woke up after that," Corn Poe said.

Beatrice and Barney ran down and jumped in, and a drum began to pound back at the campfire. Lionel pulled on his clothes, put the bear claws back around his neck and under his shirt, and went up to join the others.

The small fire had grown. The smaller children, led by Corn Poe, piled on a variety of brush, and it grew, lighting the surrounding trees with an eerie black-orange glow.

Corn Poe and Tom began to shuffle around the

fire to the drum, stopping occasionally to let out a yell of one sort or another. The rest of the children joined them, followed by Barney, who appeared out of the darkness, shivering and wet from the creek.

Lionel saw Beatrice across the fire from him, adjusting her knife on the beaded belt that hung around the long deer-skin shirt that their grandfather had made for her. Her hair was wet, and she wore a single line of the charcoal paste across her eyes like the mask of a raccoon. Lionel felt glad that she was his sister. He watched as all of the children entered the circle moving around the fire in a slow shuffle. Beatrice fell in, and Lionel watched as she got lost dancing to the slow beat of the drum and the snap of the roaring fire.

Lionel was dizzy again, but this time it was different. His mind was light, but his body was still coordinated. He joined the others, falling easily into the uncertain, irregular rhythm of the child drummer. Lionel thought about the bear in the stream and the three hawks and the eagle they had seen the first time he had gone to their grandfather's, before he had ever even heard of the boarding school. He continued to dance, thinking about Beatrice and staring lost into the fire.

Lionel was not sure how long they danced. He felt his body growing tired but continued to move. At some point he noticed Corn Poe leave the circle but watched as he returned, holding a green glass bottle. It looked like the bottle that the Frozen Man was holding when he offered the necklace.

Corn Poe pulled a cork out of the nose of the bottle, tipped it high over his head, and drank. He lowered the bottle with a grimace and let out a shrieking yelp. He handed the bottle to Tom Gunn, who drank and passed it along to Barney Little Plume. Barney drank repeatedly and then passed it to Beatrice. "I took this outta my uncle's supply. He's a bootlegger. Don't think he'll mind."

Beatrice ignored Barney, glared at Corn Poe, and continued to dance. Barney took another swig and handed it back to Tom. This continued until the bottle was empty, and Barney threw it over into the trees.

They continued to dance, and Corn Poe took to jumping over the fire, which Tom began to mimic successfully. Barney joined in, and on his fourth pass fell short, landing with a thud near the edge of the flames. He was lucky and rolled sideways, burning only some of his hair and the backside of his pants. Lionel thought about the burned leggings as Barney fell over laughing and swatting at the smoking holes in his clothes. As far as Lionel knew, Barney didn't stand up again until morning. He just sat like a potbellied stove on the edge of the shadows, either watching the dancers or turning to stare at Ulysses.

Corn Poe danced aimlessly and fell over often. He wrestled with Tom Gunn and two of the other children, and then tried to wrestle with Lionel and Beatrice. Beatrice simply threw Corn Poe away, saying, "You're certainly acting the fool." Lionel thought that Beatrice might be mad at Corn Poe.

The rest of the children continued to dance, some of them until they fell over from exhaustion, sleeping where they dropped. Corn Poe was a part of this group, and Lionel watched as Beatrice made sure that he didn't roll into the fire.

When everyone stopped dancing and the drummer stopped drumming, Beatrice drank from the rusty pail, sat down, and stared into the dying fire. Lionel did the same, as did Tom Gunn. Barney took to staring across the fire at Beatrice or the horse, his eyelids, like Lionel's, growing heavier and heavier.

Lionel watched as Barney's breathing got louder. His shoulders slumped forward, and he no longer looked like a potbellied stove but more resembled a bear that had somehow drifted off to sleep in a rocking chair. Lionel fell asleep staring at the fire, just after Tom Gunn nodded off, his chin on his chest.

When Lionel woke up he thought that his tongue had grown three times its size and that it no longer fit in his mouth. He was thirsty, his body was stiff from the dancing, and he had leaves and pine needles in his hair. Beatrice kneeled next to him, gently shaking his shoulder, her hand clasped over his mouth.

Lionel sat up and looked around to find everyone lying where he had been when the night ended. Barney had rolled over but continued to snore, and Beatrice rose to move Corn Poe's foot, which was once again dangerously close to the fading embers of the previous night.

Beatrice motioned Lionel to the creek. He crawled to his feet and stumbled through the trees to the bank, where he dropped to his knees and drank. The water was good and cold, and he drank until he could no longer take the blood rushing to his head.

When Lionel looked up from the water, Beatrice was standing above him with Ulysses's reins in her hands. She led the horse into the creek and slipped onto his back. Lionel did the same, and they walked the horse downstream. They hadn't gone a hundred paces when Beatrice stopped the horse.

"You're not coming with us," Beatrice said without turning her head.

Lionel looked back, and there was Corn Poe. Like Lionel, with leaves and pine needles in his hair, black soot face paint smeared from sleep.

"I'll bet I am," Corn Poe said.

Beatrice pulled up the horse and growled, "No, you're not. We can't have ya and you don't need to get involved in horse thievin'. You said yerself, they're liable to hang us."

"You best to let me come, or I'll scream and wake up the whole damn lot of 'em."

Beatrice thought about this. "Go ahead, wake 'em. What concern of that is mine?"

"I was just thinkin' that if you could avoid a confrontation with Barney over that horse that you might. You sure don't want him up and ready to follow ya wherever we're going."

Beatrice didn't answer, but turned the horse and reached out to pull the boy up behind her. "Ya gonna do what I say?"

"Of course!" Corn Poe said, his face an ear-to-ear grin. Lionel supposed that if Beatrice was mad at Corn Poe for drinking the corn liquor, this marked the point where she got over it.

They rode downstream, and at some point Beatrice, confident that they had thrown off Barney, turned Ulysses, and they rode back around the Great Wood toward the mountains.

Chapter Twenty-Four

Asleep in the Woods • Corn Poe's Declaration • A Visitor

Sometime near morning they stopped and slept in the crux of a large fallen tree and the base of a living one. Lionel slept soundly but was woken midday by a cardinal that fluttered from branch to branch to branch in the trees overhead.

It was dark when they stopped, so their surroundings seemed foreign to him, but he didn't feel out of place. Lionel figured that they were somewhere in the heart of the Great Wood, less than a half day's ride or so from their lodge in the meadow.

He got up from his pine-needle bed and carefully crossed to scratch Ulysses's long face. Corn Poe slept nestled up against Beatrice, snoring soundly.

Corn Poe looked dirty, the soot from the night before still smeared all over his face. Beatrice's black

ash mask, however, remained intact and looked as natural as if she had been born with it.

Lionel got a flask of water, the smoked meat, and the berries from the bundle they had tied around Ulysses's withers. He sat in the pine needles eating the berries, surrounded by the giant trees, watching Corn Poe and his sister sleep. Beatrice's buckskin shirt blended into the base of the tree and the pine needles that were strewn all around them. Lionel thought that if the soldiers were looking for them, it wouldn't be hard for them to disappear.

The wind picked up, knocking a dead branch from high above, and the cracking sounds it made as it crashed onto the forest floor woke both Beatrice and Corn Poe. Beatrice's eyes shot open; she coughed, then stared at Lionel, who sat cross-legged in the midst of the Great Wood, watching her.

Corn Poe sat up and immediately grabbed ahold of his head with both hands, proclaiming, "If I had me a hatchet, I think I'd just do myself a favor and cut this sucker right off at the neck."

"I know where we got one not too far from here," Beatrice said, pushing Corn Poe off of her.

"Ah, it's not funny," Corn Poe moaned, rolling

over in the pine needles. "My head hurts something awful."

Lionel got up and brought him one of the water sacks. He handed Beatrice the bundle of berries and meat. She opened it and ate while they both watched Corn Poe flail on the ground and listened to his moaning proclamations denouncing liquor from this moment forward. Corn Poe swore that he would never touch the stuff again as long as he lived, a statement that Lionel and Beatrice doubted.

Beatrice told Corn Poe to drink the water and that if he wanted to eat he should. They would be leaving soon. Corn Poe got up and wandered a ways into the woods. He returned with a large pinecone that he gave to Beatrice and thanked her for allowing him to travel with them.

"It wasn't my intention," was Beatrice's reply.

The children finished their breakfast and continued their journey back toward the lodge. They walked, leading the horse for the majority of the day, enjoying the cool shade of the Great Wood. Sometime that afternoon they arrived at the tree-lined perimeter of their meadow, but froze when they saw a strange horse grazing in front of the lodge's crooked door.

Part Three

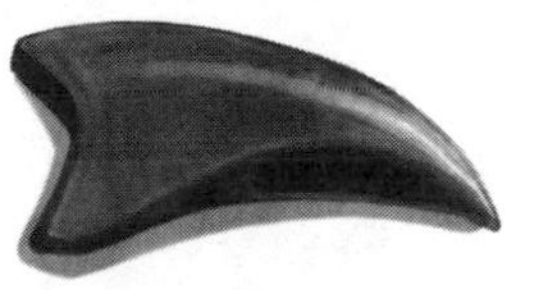

THE FIRST thing that Avery John Hawkins and the boy noticed when they returned to the lodge in the meadow was the garden. It was thick and looked as if it was about to burst from the original rectangular patch that the children and their grandfather plotted. Fat green tomatoes sagged on their vines. Watermelon, cucumbers, and squash crept forward, spilling into the tall grass of the meadow. The pole beans stood well over the straw man's head, leaving the ghostly figure to stand in his silk dress, idly watching as the beanstalks slowly strangled the sunflowers.

Hawkins stepped up to the straw man and ran a thick finger over the tight weave and the feathers that fluttered around its head in the late afternoon breeze. He looked around at the trampled grass between him and the unearthed smokehouse.

"Maybe you should wait up in the woods while I have a look around," he said to the boy. "I know that I ain't seen no one here for two days, but it still don't feel right."

Avery John Hawkins pulled a rifle wrapped in beaded buckskin from the side of his horse and turned the boy toward the woods.

"Now, you keep your eyes open, and if it comes to it, don't be afraid to flash your Winchester like I taught ya."

The boy turned his horse and the pack mule and headed toward the stream and the far side of the woods. Hawkins crossed the meadow and stood in front of the crooked lodge, staring at the sagging door.

He looked around the meadow again, then pushed the door open and stepped inside. Hawkins had grown accustomed to returning to the lodge to find it in some state of disarray no matter what improvements he and the boy had made during their brief stays there. Animals of some sort seemed to always find their way in, leaving their mark as they saw fit. In particular, Hawkins thought of the wolverine that he often found inside and had yet to figure out its point of entry. Hawkins proceeded with caution, half expecting the creature to jump out at him with every step.

The lodge was now neatly stocked with a variety of provisions. In a far corner, arrows and bows stood in various stages of completion, and there were hides adorned with beadwork and bundles of feathers. Vegetables, some fresher than others, hung from the rafters, leading Hawkins's eye to the support beams which now stood under the lodge's sagging roof.

Avery John Hawkins shifted the heavy rifle in his hand and thought about how long it had been since he and the boy had been able to stay in one place longer than a couple of days. He knew that if they could, this is where he would like to settle, but he quickly dismissed the thought and checked to see how well the boy was hiding himself in the woods.

He stood at the thick glass window near the fireplace, running his eyes across the tree line and the garden, thinking that he had taught the boy well. The boy was nowhere to be seen. He leaned closer to the window and his heavy breathing steamed the glass, revealing a handprint. A print that was no bigger than the boy's.

A flash of movement caught the corner of Avery John Hawkins's eye. He stepped back from the window and peered deep into the woods.

Chapter Twenty-Five

Corn Poe Drops the Reins • A Scuffle • Shots Fired • Greetings • Junebug • The Lodge

LIONEL STRAINED his eyes as best he could, but no matter how hard he tried, he could no longer see Beatrice. He knew that she was somewhere toward the edge of the woods, not twenty paces or so ahead, but to the eye, she was gone.

"You can't spot her, huh?" Corn Poe whispered.

"Shhh. Beatrice said not to say nothing," Lionel insisted.

"Oh, I can still see her," Corn Poe went on. "I got what they call the eagle eye."

Corn Poe's eyes darted from side to side, tree-to-tree. Lionel didn't believe him. He was sure that Corn Poe had lost sight of her about the same time as he had, if not sooner. If Beatrice didn't want to be seen, she would not be seen.

"We should just stay here with Ulysses like Beatrice said," Lionel whispered, turning back to the horse—but Ulysses was gone.

Lionel whipped around to see that Ulysses was wandering toward the meadow and the strange horse that stood grazing in front of their lodge.

"The reins," Lionel stammered to Corn Poe. "You were supposed to hold the reins."

Corn Poe spun around. "Where the hell does he think he's off to?"

"Beatrice told you to hold the reins. Where are you going?" Lionel asked.

"To get Ulysses."

"But she told us not to move."

"Well, which is it? Were we supposed to watch the horse or not move? 'Cause the horse, he's movin'!" Corn Poe took off, trailing Ulysses, who was getting closer and closer to the tree line at the edge of the meadow. Lionel followed.

Ulysses made his way through the low brush and across the meadow. He stopped and nudged the strange horse with his long nose. The strange horse did the same, and then the two horses took to standing next to each other, calmly ripping up the grass.

Lionel and Corn Poe crouched at the edge of the Great Wood, watching the horses.

"What in the hell are they doing?" Corn Poe whispered.

"I suppose they're bein' social," Lionel offered, "but Ulysses shouldn't be out there in the first place. You were supposed to hold him."

"Well, what do you want me to do now?" Corn Poe pleaded through clenched teeth.

"We'll wait," Lionel told the older boy with authority.

They crawled on their bellies through the scrub, following a series of broken and decaying timber to where the tree line came closest to the lodge. That's when they saw Beatrice.

She appeared from the far side of the meadow and in a crouched run was soon standing at Ulysses's side. The big warhorse nuzzled her with his long head and let out a loud whinny. When the other horse responded, the shadow of a man appeared, ducking under the crooked doorframe of the lodge. Beatrice slipped behind Ulysses and the man's horse, but there was nowhere good for her to hide.

The man scanned the perimeter of the Great Wood and then stepped back into the darkness of the lodge. Beatrice took the opportunity to swing up onto Ulysses's back, but before she could turn the horse, the man sprang from the shadows of the lodge and in two running steps had Ulysses by the harness. The man's horse spun violently from the commotion.

Beatrice pulled back on the reins, trying in vain to free Ulysses, who instead sidestepped, mimicking the other horse, dragging the man and throwing Beatrice from his back: a sight that Lionel had never before seen. Beatrice and the man tumbled into each other as Ulysses and the other horse bolted from the lodge toward the edge of the woods. The man rolled over and in a flurry of movement was on top of Beatrice.

Lionel froze at the edge of the wood until Corn Poe broke him from his stupor.

"That sonuvabitch is fixin' to kill your sister!" Corn Poe proclaimed, and then burst forward from their cover and ran screaming toward the man and Beatrice, who struggled in the high grass.

Without thinking, Lionel followed; and before he knew it, had joined Corn Poe on the man's back. The man tried to shake the two boys with a series of bucking motions, but did not find success until he reached around and grabbed hold of first Corn Poe and then Lionel. He yanked the two screaming boys from his back and threw them to the side, where they rolled toward the sag of the crooked doorframe.

Corn Poe scrambled to his feet, brandishing the small wooden stool that Grandpa had sat on while making the straw man. He raised it high over his head as though he aimed to bring it down, if possible, through the man's skull.

"Now, hold on!" the man shouted, still pinning Beatrice to the ground but craning his neck sideways to keep an eye on Corn Poe and Lionel.

Corn Poe lifted the stool higher but was interrupted by a shot that rang like thunder across the small valley. The four of them froze and looked toward the woods and the cloud of black, burning gunpowder that rose from the barrel of a large rifle held by a small boy on horseback.

"Let's all just hold on," the man repeated, trying to catch his breath and loosening his grip on Beatrice.

The small boy rode across the meadow, his gun

pointed directly at Corn Poe.

"Now why don't you put that there stool down and we can talk, okay?" said the man.

The boy reached the front of the lodge and pulled his horse to a stop, the rifle still trained on Corn Poe.

"Everyone agree? Then, if you still want to put that stool through my head, you're more than welcome to try it. What'a say? We can talk, huh?" the man repeated.

Beatrice motioned to Corn Poe, who answered by lowering the stool.

"Now, for starters, some names. My name is Hawkins, Avery John Hawkins, and that there is my boy Joshua, but he goes by the name of Junebug."

"Junebug Hawkins? What the hell kinda name is that?" Corn Poe eyed the boy on the horse. "Sounds made up if you ask me."

"Made up? Well, all names are made up at some point and be that as it may, that's his name." Avery John Hawkins stood and extended his hand.

Lionel looked up at him for the first time and realized that he was different from the men at the outpost. To start, his skin was dark like his and Beatrice's, darker, actually, and his hair at its peak sat about six inches from the top of his head. It wasn't straight like his or Beatrice's, either, but clung wildly in dry, tight curls, reminding Lionel of the tuft of hair on the mounted buffalo head that hung in the captain's office.

Lionel took Mr. Hawkins's big hand. "I'm Lionel. That's my sister, Beatrice, and that there is Corn Poe, Corn Poe Boss Ribs."

"And Junebug Hawkins sounds made up?" Hawkins said, smiling. "Nice to meet you, Corn Poe."

"My name ain't made up. It's what my paps calls me," Corn Poe said, still eyeing Junebug and the rifle with suspicion.

"Why, come on down, son, and put the rifle away," Mr. Hawkins said to the boy he called Junebug. Then, turning to Beatrice, he extended his hand once again, which Beatrice reluctantly took hold of, and Hawkins pulled her to her feet.

"Sorry about that, Beatrice, right? I thought you were fixin' to take old Mr. Hawkins's horse or worse."

Beatrice stood, collecting herself. Lionel watched her, amazed at how small she looked next to Mr.

Hawkins. He was a big man, almost the same size as Corn Poe's father, but not as wide.

"Now, it's gettin' late. If we can agree to be friends, maybe we could get some supper goin'." Mr. Hawkins rested a hand on his son's shoulder. "Then we'll figure out what we're all doin' in each other's lodge."

Chapter Twenty-Six

Hawkins's Biscuits • Elk Dog • Trust

Avery John Hawkins crouched beside a small fire pounding dough in his large hands. He dropped the dough as biscuits into the bacon grease that popped and hissed in the blackened skillet.

"I tell ya. During these summer months I do prefer to stay out of doors as long as the weather permits," Mr. Hawkins said, dropping another biscuit into the pan. "It helps during them long winter months, when that cold got you froze clear to the bone."

Mr. Hawkins looked at the sprawl of stars that spread across the inky black night.

"You stop and think to yourself, It sure is cold now, but I do remember a warm summer evening not too long ago, and that does what it can to stove off the night," Hawkins continued. "Even just for the moment, it surely does."

There was something to Mr. Hawkins's voice that Lionel had never heard before. Something foreign that didn't sound like any of the Blackfeet or government people that occupied the outpost.

"Say, there, Corn Poe. You mind keepin' an eye on them biscuits for a minute? I want to check on the corn." Hawkins smiled. "I wanna check on the *corn*, Corn Poe."

Mr. Hawkins reached barehanded into the fire and rotated the five ears of corn that lay in their blackened husks at the edge of the glowing ash. "I usually like to soak the corn for a day or so before roasting. Helps lock in some of that flavor." Then Mr. Hawkins turned his attention to the brook trout that he'd instructed Junebug to pull from the stream earlier. There were five good-sized fish, stuffed with wild onions from the banks of the stream, skewered and hanging over the dancing flames. "That should be enough, well, with maybe some melon for dessert—that is, if you don't mind gettin' one from the garden there, Lionel."

Lionel looked to Beatrice before leaving the circle of firelight. He wasn't sure what to make of their new guests. Beatrice nodded, but did not take her eyes from the man and his son.

Lionel walked toward the garden. The cool grass was wet with the night and felt good on his bare feet. The smells from the Hawkinses' cook fire urged him to move quickly.

"Joint guests is what we are." Mr. Hawkins's voice carried across the meadow. "We're enjoying the fruits of your labor and what you done to the place, and y'all gettin' ready to sample the culinary wiles of the Hawkinses, firsthand."

Lionel paused to let his eyes adjust to the darkness before stepping from the grass into the turned earth of the garden. He looked up at the countless stars and listened to the crashing movement of the stream in the distance.

"How come this fellow over here, *Junebug* as you call him, never says nothin'?" Lionel heard Corn Poe ask. "I seem to notice that you're the one doin' all the talkin'."

"Oh, Junebug will say plenty if you listen," Hawkins said without turning from the flames, "but he don't have the words that you or I have. He's a mute."

"Mute. Well, I suppose that would explain it,"

Corn Poe said, looking to Junebug and then suddenly raising his voice. "I just thought you was rude or somethin'!"

Mr. Hawkins let out a long, bellowing laugh that was soon accompanied by a strange but similar version of the same laugh from Junebug. It was the first sound that any of them had heard from the boy since they had met him at gunpoint late that afternoon.

"Why, he's mute. He can't talk. That don't mean he's *deaf*," Mr. Hawkins said through his laughter. "I don't mean to chuckle, but we've seen it done before. The few people we see, always raisin' their voices when they hear that he don't speak like we do, when there's no need. He hears better than any of us do, but people always want to raise their voices when they talk to him. Ain't that right, Junebug?"

Junebug nodded his head in agreement, his strange laugh bubbling into a slight giggle. As Lionel returned from the darkness with a large melon, he noticed that Beatrice's face had slipped into a smile, and that even Corn Poe couldn't help but laugh, despite the laughter being somewhat at his own expense. Lionel figured that Corn Poe may have become accustomed to this position.

"And Mr. Lionel with the melon. That sure looks like a good one. Here, boy, let's set it over there." Hawkins took the melon and laid it next to his saddle by the fire and then, raising his voice to thunderous proportions: "Or should I say over there!"

They all settled around the fire to eat, but continued to giggle and take turns speaking in the loud manner in which Corn Poe had addressed Junebug. The tension that had occupied the afternoon and early evening seemed to erode, and even Beatrice took a turn, asking, rather loudly at one point, for Lionel to pass her another piece of freshly cut melon. This brought relieved laughter from Mr. Hawkins most of all, and after they had all finished, they settled back in the grass around the fire and looked up at the endless sea of stars.

"Oh, man, that was some good eatin' there, Mr. Hawkins," Corn Poe announced. "I was as hungry as a horse, but now I feel like a swolled-up tick a-fixin' to pop."

"Yes, it was, and I'd like to thank all of y'all for havin' me and the boy," Mr. Hawkins added. "I didn't know what to think when I saw old Beatrice there sneaking up to my horse dressed the way y'all's dressed. I ain't seen no Indians in clothes like that in some time. You must be from the Blackfeet rez down below, huh?"

"Yes, sir, we are. But we're renegades, on account of them trying to force the Blackfeet outta us," Corn Poe declared.

"I do know that feelin'," Mr. Hawkins answered, reaching for a small leather bag and pulling from it a pipe that he packed with tobacco.

"Hey, our grandpa smokes a pipe like that," Lionel observed, then looked to Beatrice for approval.

"Is that right?" Mr. Hawkins asked, lighting the pipe. The big man sat smoking, his knees fixed to the insides of his elbows, staring off, lost in the fire.

It was quiet for some time, and Lionel thought that he might have dozed off for a minute. It had been a long day, and one that was not to be forgotten. Lionel was startled by a soft whinny that he recognized to be Ulysses, who was resting somewhere in the darkness of the meadow surrounding them. The Hawkinses' horses answered, and then they all seemed to settle back down around the fire.

"That's a helluva horse," Mr. Hawkins said, breaking what passed for silence in the meadow with the distant sound of the stream, the wind in the Great

Wood, and the crickets that sang softly in the high grass.

"That there is Ulysses, the fastest horse in all of Montana," Corn Poe said, drawing a heavy glare from Beatrice. "What? He is!"

"You don't say," Mr. Hawkins continued, noticing Beatrice's scowl. "I suppose it ain't none of my business how y'all came by a horse like that, but it sure is good lookin'."

Mr. Hawkins leaned forward and took a drink of cool stream water from a tin cup and spat in the fire. "You said y'all was Blackfeet? Piegan, eh? Niitsítapi—the original people. The real people."

"That's right," Corn Poe said, with perhaps more to prove on the subject than Beatrice or Lionel.

"You know I was down there for a while. Back when I was with the army, Tenth Cavalry." Mr. Hawkins threw another piece of wood on the fire. "Why, I've been told that it was you Blackfeet that first domesticated the horse. Called 'em '*po-no-kah-mita.*' You know what that means?"

"No, can't say that I do," Corn Poe answered for the group, careful to avert his eyes from Beatrice's close and cautious glare.

"Y'all don't speak it, eh? Well, *po-no-kah-mita* is Blackfeet for 'elk-dog.' Big as an elk, but you're able to work 'em, carrying loads, like dogs."

Mr. Hawkins leaned back against his saddle and took a long draw on his pipe, his dark face streaked with dancing firelight.

"Yep, the Blackfeet are known as some of the greatest horsemen the plains have ever seen—that much is true."

"Some?" Corn Poe spat, once again looking to Beatrice for support.

Ulysses and the Hawkinses' horses appeared out of the darkness as though they had been listening all along.

"*Nioomítaa* . . . A great horse," Mr. Hawkins concluded, looking up at the horses.

Lionel rolled over onto his side and studied Beatrice. She was the best horseman he had ever seen, and today he had seen that even she could get thrown off by the "elk-dog." A jumpy elk-dog named Ulysses.

Chapter Twenty-Seven

Cold Morning Dew • Fishing the Stream • Red Blood • Starfish

Lionel stared up into an early-morning sky. Purple, yellow, orange, and gold all combined and stretched across the faint light from tree line to tree line. Lionel felt the weight of his grandfather's buffalo robe over him and wondered how it had gotten there, as it hadn't been around him when Mr. Hawkins was talking about the horses.

Lionel threw off the robe, even heavier now that it was wet with the morning dew. He sat up and looked over at Corn Poe and Junebug. They were still sleeping, wrapped now in the saddle blankets and some bedrolls that Lionel figured must have belonged to the Hawkinses. Beatrice and Mr. Hawkins were nowhere to be found.

He wandered over toward their crude outhouse, took care of his business, and then cut back across the meadow, past the garden and toward the stream. The meadow was also wet with the morning, and in a few short steps his bare feet and the bottom cuffs of his leggings were soaked. Lionel looked with pride at their little garden and saw that the black raven he had seen when they first arrived at the little lodge had returned and was sitting on the straw man's shoulder, busily working on one of the pearl buttons of the ivory dress.

"Hello, again," Lionel called, but the black bird ignored him, concentrating on his task at hand.

The raven pecked and pulled relentlessly until he had the shiny button in his beak; then looked at Lionel with a cold black eye and flew away, disappearing somewhere over the Great Wood. Lionel continued on to the stream to see if the grizzly bear that he and his grandfather had seen fishing had been through during the last couple of days.

Lionel walked up the rise to the stream and found Beatrice standing waist deep in one of the pools, peering, with her arm half-cocked, into the swirling water. Mr. Hawkins was standing above her on the bank, tying off what looked like the back of a wicker chair, made from the rough whittled branches of slippery elm and pine boughs.

"Ya see, I'll simply slip this on the downward side of the stream, and what do ya know? They're trapped," Lionel heard Mr. Hawkins say over the rush of water. He set his weaving into the water, blocking its downward flow. "They ain't got nowheres to go but back upstream, and that is something I'd like to see, with you standing there just waitin' on 'em."

Mr. Hawkins looked up, instinctively reaching for the large pistol that he wore in his belt, but immediately dropping his hand when he saw that it was Lionel standing on the shore.

"Beatrice, look who's come to join us," Mr. Hawkins shouted over the water as he danced from rock to rock, crossing the stream to Lionel. "How did you sleep last night, Lionel? I slept like the rock of Gibraltar, myself. No joke, like the rock of Gibraltar."

Mr. Hawkins pulled the pistol from his belt and sat down on the soft, moss-covered bank. He threw down his heavy saddlebag and pulled a small black notebook from inside.

"Now, give me a minute here, Lionel, I just need to make a note. This crick here seems to change course a bit every time I see it," Mr. Hawkins said, setting the narrow nub of a crude pencil to the page. "That's water for ya, though, ain't it? It'll find a way to go where it wants to go. Not much you can do about that, not much at all."

Lionel looked over Hawkins's shoulder at the scribbled notes and various rough penciled sketches of trees, rocks, and animals that covered the open pages.

"I'm not sure why, but I do like to make notes of me and the Junebug's travels. I'm hoping we won't always be on the move like this, and if we do settle back down, I keep thinking that he may want to recall some of what we've seen."

Lionel saw that Mr. Hawkins's latest chronicle was a drawing of the brook trout that they had had for dinner and a sketch of the stream and its various pools that were laid out directly before them. Lionel sat down next to Mr. Hawkins, and Hawkins handed him a canteen. "Have a drink of that. Just filled from the stream. That's good cold water."

Lionel took hold of the canteen and drank. Mr.

Hawkins was right. The cold water felt good going down his throat, and he drank it in greedy gulps.

"Well, now, there's a way to catch a fish that I ain't thought of; maybe you could just drink up all the stream's water and then we could just walk on out there and pick them fish up," Mr. Hawkins said, breaking the lead on his pencil before finishing his sketch. "Good Lord, I've got to find a way to get some more pencils. This one is about done."

Lionel looked up at his sister, who stood patiently in the stream as Mr. Hawkins pulled a small jackknife from his pocket, flipped open the blade, and worked on getting the last bit of lead from what remained of the pencil.

"I'm hoping to get a couple more weeks outta this one yet," Mr. Hawkins said, maybe more to the pencil than Lionel. "Just a bit more . . ."

But the pocketknife slipped, sliding into Mr. Hawkins's finger instead of the pencil's soft wood.

"Will you look at that?" Mr. Hawkins announced dropping the pencil and knife and examining his finger. "I cut myself."

A small trickle of blood, red blood, Lionel noticed, appeared on Mr. Hawkins's thick finger. It fell in tiny droplets onto the green moss where they sat.

"Ah, it's just a tiny cut, but all the same. That little pencil sure is making me work for it, ain't that right, Lionel?" Mr. Hawkins asked, wiping the blood onto his pants.

Lionel stared at the faint blood-streaked lines across Mr. Hawkins's trousers and the dark red droplets that sat in half bubbles on the clumps of moss around their outstretched legs.

"What is it, boy? You ain't squeamish on a little blood, are ya?"

"No, sir," Lionel explained. "I just didn't figure on yer blood being red like mine."

Mr. Hawkins looked puzzled for a moment, his face slowly slipping into a big grin. "Why, of course my blood is red." Mr. Hawkins laughed. "What color did you expect it to be? Purple, or maybe green?"

"No," Lionel stammered, "I guess I just didn't know. I mean your skin's different than ours."

"My skin, oh my goodness, my skin." Hawkins coughed through his boisterous laughter. "No, Lionel, I'm sorry. I suppose you're right. How would ya know unless ya seen it?"

Mr. Hawkins found this to be rather amusing and

it took him some time to control his laughter. "Ya know, Lionel, I suppose I should take it as a good sign that ya ain't never seen none of our blood."

Mr. Hawkins went back to sharpening the pencil between small bursts of steady laughter. "In all my travels, that's the first on that one. Red blood."

"Where are ya from, Mr. Hawkins?" Lionel asked as Mr. Hawkins's laughter subsided.

"Why, that's a good question, Lionel. I'm from a bit of the all-over, really," Mr. Hawkins answered, slowly exposing the remaining lead. "I know that things have changed down where you're from, but the fact remains that you're still *from* there. Your people been here for a long time. My people, whoever they are, been scattered all over the world."

"So, you don't know where you're from?" Lionel persisted.

"Well, kinda. I ended up here outta Texas. Like I was sayin', I was with the army and now, on this particular mountain, well that's a whole other story. Before Texas, I was on the coast in the Carolinas, back east. Before that, I know that my mother was born down in the islands, somewhere's south of Cuba. You can hear a bit of that in my voice, I reckon, but not too much anymore. Ya know a long, long time ago I hear that my folks is from some part of Africa, but I ain't never been there."

Mr. Hawkins leaned over and pulled his saddle-bag closer. "I suppose I don't know which is worse, being taken from the place you're from or having where you're from taken from you. Either way, it's a sorry state of affairs that we both better learn to make the best of 'cause it ain't gonna change. It's done, and that ol' clock ain't gonna turn itself back."

Mr. Hawkins threw open the flap of his saddle-bag and fished around until he found a small, well-worn wooden box. "Let me show you something."

Mr. Hawkins opened the box and removed an object that was wrapped in red silk. Lionel thought at first that it was some sort of strangely shaped rock.

"Here ya go," Mr. Hawkins said, "but be careful with it. My mother gave me that. It's from the island where she was born."

Lionel took it from Hawkins and held it gingerly in his hand. It was as hard as a rock but as light as a pinecone. It had five stubby appendages surrounding its center, and when Lionel turned it over, he noticed a hole in the middle that could have very well been a mouth. Surrounding the mouth and trailing out of each limb, there were hundreds if not thousands of what looked like hairs, orange hairs: little orange hairs, with a mouth that had turned to stone.

"You know what it is?" Mr. Hawkins asked.

"No, I never seen nothin' like it."

"It's the knobby star, *Piaster giganteus*."

"Piaster giganteus?"

"Yeah, it's a starfish."

Lionel turned it over in his hand again. "This is a fish?"

"Kind of."

"This was alive?"

"Yep, just like you and me. They live in the salt-water down in the oceans. You ever seen an ocean?"

"No, but I seen pictures back at the school. The captain told me that they're so big you can't see the other side. I saw a picture of the army men on the boats. They was fixin' to cross 'em."

"Yeah, I'll bet they were," Mr. Hawkins said.

"How did it die?" Lionel asked.

"How did what die?"

"The starfish."

"I don't know 'cause I wasn't there, but I reckon it was like these fish here that we pull outta the stream. Sometimes when you take something out of where or how it's supposed to be, it'll just . . . well . . . it just dies."

"Everything?"

"Naw, not everything, some things change, they adapt," Hawkins said, taking the starfish back and wrapping it in the red silk handkerchief.

"Can I look at the starfish again some time?"

"Why, of course you can. Whenever you like, as long as you're careful. It means a lot to me as it's the only thing I got left that my mother ever give me, well exceptin' the purple and green blood that flows through these veins." Mr. Hawkins laughed.

Lionel looked upstream to his sister. Beatrice reached down, submerging herself in the pool, then resurfaced with a flapping brook trout in her bare hands. It reminded Lionel of the time that he and his grandfather had sat in this very spot and watched the grizzly bear do the same.

CHAPTER TWENTY-EIGHT

COLD BISCUITS • WINTER STORES • PIRATES AND THE EXPLORERS OF AFRICA • AN AGREEMENT

FOR THE NEXT half hour, Beatrice pulled fish with greater frequency. Lionel stood observing from the shore while Mr. Hawkins went back up to the lodge to get the cook fire going. Lionel watched the growing number of fish as they lay packed in moss, gasping for their final breath. He had enjoyed the fish the night before and knew that he would eat them again for breakfast, but now, after seeing the starfish, he did so with an awareness that wasn't present until this morning.

Lionel thought about his grandfather and wondered when he would return. He wondered what his grandfather would think of the starfish and these new thoughts that now raced through his head. Lionel decided that he would say a prayer thanking the fish for their lives. He sat down on the bank with one hand on the bear claws around his neck and sang a low song.

Beatrice caught another fish, threw it up on the bank, and then crossed the pool to join Lionel. He thought about stopping the song and telling Beatrice about the starfish, but instead he kept singing, and they were soon joined by Junebug and Corn Poe, who appeared on the opposite bank looking disheveled and wiping the night from their eyes. Lionel grew quiet.

"I'm thinkin' that a swim is the only thing that's gonna get me goin' after a sleep like that," Corn Poe announced, stripping off his clothes.

Beatrice gathered the fish, smiled at Lionel, and disappeared in the direction of the lodge.

"I suppose that's right, leave the bathing hour to the menfolk. It's only proper," Corn Poe continued, slipping into the icy pool. Junebug followed, then Lionel; and soon the three of them were swimming where their breakfast had just been caught.

They ate the fish with cold biscuits and spent the rest of the day looking over and repairing the

Hawkinses' gear. Mr. Hawkins showed them their traps and the pelts and skins they had gathered over the course of the long winter. Lionel and Beatrice told Mr. Hawkins what their grandfather had taught them, and he soon put them to work in the smokehouse curing the meat and tanning the hides that lay in bundles, bent and tied in stiff squares.

This continued for the rest of August, with the five of them falling into a pleasant routine that felt the most settled since Beatrice and Lionel had fled the school. They spent the days preparing the lodge for winter, tanning the hides, smoking meat, and preserving the vegetables from their overflowing garden and the abundant huckleberries, blackberries, blueberries, and raspberries that began to cover the hills.

They saw the grizzly bear with greater frequency as he also chose to spend his late-summer afternoons in the berry patches eating his fill for the long winter that lay ahead. They also took walks in the Great Wood, sometimes to hunt, but mainly just to take in, as Mr. Hawkins put it, "its magnificence."

This strange consortium sat around the fire at night always in the open air, and Mr. Hawkins told them stories from the war, the Carolinas, and the few tales of piracy and the high seas that he still remembered from his mother's island.

Lionel loved these times and grew closer and closer to Corn Poe and the mute boy, Junebug. They often stole away in the afternoons after their chores were done to act out Mr. Hawkins's tales of piracy or to fish and swim in the stream.

They found a sprawling section of fallen trees in the Great Wood that became one of their favorite spots. There, they would engage the pillaging pirates or the gruff sea captains that hunted them down, depending on what Hawkins's tales and that day's imagination dictated. A clearing opened onto a broken jumble of giant tumbled trees now lying dead and dying in star-shaped patterns stretching as far as their eyes could see. Lionel loved to run along their immense trunks and climb through their extensive branches, which, while still perpendicular to their base, reached up as opposed to out, their tips in some cases as high as the standing trees that still surrounded them. The fallen trees' exposed roots were now the bows of great ships, the extending branches their masts and rigging. Corn Poe thought that they could walk the trunks all the way to Canada and never have to touch the ground.

When they weren't engaged in piracy on the high seas of the Great Wood, they wandered the rocky crags that surrounded the small lodge in the meadow, pretending to be lost somewhere in the ancient wilds of Africa—not recognizing themselves for the pioneers and explorers that they really were.

As the nights became colder Mr. Hawkins suggested that they sleep indoors around the crumbled fireplace, although he continued to sleep out of doors, the pistol and rifle always at his side.

Beatrice seemed happy, but also became more withdrawn. She slept inside with them, but as the cool weather approached, her coughing returned; and many nights Lionel would wake to find her sitting upright and staring into the fire, trying to catch her breath, or standing at the lodge's thick-glassed windows, looking out into the night sky.

One morning they woke to find Mr. Hawkins and his bedroll covered in a light powder of snow, but the snow had all but melted by mid-morning, and the day turned out no different from the rest of these last days of summer. Beatrice agreed with Mr. Hawkins that they could all stay in the little meadow as long as they worked together and didn't ask each other too many questions about why they each needed to stay there instead of moving to a more suitable climate.

On the morning of the second snow, they awoke to find Mr. Hawkins covered in another light dusting. He was sitting by the open-air fire, talking to their grandfather.

Chapter Twenty-Nine

News from the Outpost • Lionel's Feather • The Best of Times • The Return of Tom Gunn

Their grandfather had been wandering the foothills and mountains for a week, trying to shake the scouts that the army post had sent to the Milk River to spy on him. He did this for two days and then circled back after what would appear to have been a satisfactory hunt but was actually a concerted attempt to keep the government men guessing as to what his recent forays into the mountains were really about. By his third attempt, he had successfully lost them within a day, but he'd continued to wander for the past week to ensure that they weren't following him to the lodge in the meadow.

Lionel was so happy to see his grandfather that he felt as though he had actually flown from the crooked door to where Grandpa sat with Mr. Hawkins at the fire.

"I see yer still growin'," Grandpa laughed, as Beatrice, Corn Poe, and Junebug joined them. "I might have mistaken you for a wild band of low-down dirty renegades if I didn't know better.

"And you," Grandpa said, placing his big hand on Corn Poe's head, "I should'a known I'd find you here."

Corn Poe squirmed joyously from the attention.

"Why didn't y'all tell me you was his kin?" Mr. Hawkins asked, handing their grandfather a tin cup of coffee.

"Hell, I've known ol' Avery John Hawkins since before all of you were even born," Grandpa said, accepting the coffee.

Grandpa explained that he and Mr. Hawkins knew each other a long time ago when Mr. Hawkins first came to Montana with the government. Then he told Mr. Hawkins about the troubles that waited for them below, and that Mr. Hawkins was sworn to secrecy, to which Hawkins nodded.

Grandpa informed them all that the government was still frantically searching for the prize horse

Ulysses, despite the approaching winter. Grandpa suspected that the search was being spearheaded and driven by Jenkins and Lumpkin.

Rumors were circulating through the outpost that a group of boys from Heart Butte had supposedly seen the horse, but that last they heard, Beatrice and Lionel were heading to Canada. This led to an exhaustive search that yielded little result, leaving Sergeant Jenkins more irate and suspicious than ever. Grandpa also said that the reward for the return of the horse had been raised to $100 cash money, and that this had him concerned as to what their next move should be.

Corn Poe inquired about his family and their reaction to his decision to run away and join a ruthless band of renegades. Grandpa seemed to be trying to soften the blow a bit, but told him that Big Bull, after a series of rants and raves, had given up on the boy and figured him dead.

"Well, you told him that I was a notorious outlaw running with a gang of miserable horse thieves, didn't ya?" Corn Poe pushed, borrowing some language from one of Mr. Hawkins's pirate tales.

"No, I said nothing to that effect. As far as I'm

concerned, I don't know what's happened to any of you," Grandpa answered, which set Corn Poe to sulking, but only as long as his attention could bear to fixate on one subject.

Beatrice and Lionel eagerly showed off their accomplishments in their grandfather's absence. They showed him their firewood stores, the late summer abundance of the garden, and the fish trap.

Grandpa stood over the stream, impressed with the tight weave of branches, but he appeared to be lost in thought.

"I'm not sure that the Suyitapis would like this," Grandpa said, packing his pipe.

"The Suyitapis?" Lionel asked.

"The underwater people. Spirits. Out of respect the old ones taught us not to disturb their world. You're old enough now so I'll leave it to you to decide."

Beatrice stared deep into the swirling pool as Mr. Hawkins, Junebug, and Corn Poe appeared on the upper bank.

"Always something to learn," Mr. Hawkins said as he made the note in his book. "Yes indeed, always something."

Lionel thought about this and decided he would

respect the old ones' way. Beatrice must have agreed, because the next time Lionel returned to the stream, he noticed that the fish trap had been dismantled and the sticks neatly stacked on the shore.

Grandpa fit easily into the renegades' routine, and this odd assembly continued making preparations for winter and enjoying each other's company on these last of the long, sun-filled days. The days grew shorter and the evening snows more frequent, with the tops of the surrounding mountain peaks already covered until next spring.

The group sat around the open campfire at night telling stories and taking in the last of this season's stars. Grandpa joined them on their long expeditions, hunting or otherwise, into the Great Wood. On one particular trip, he appeared suddenly under the great canopy and presented Lionel with an eagle feather.

"He musta wanted me to give it to you," Grandpa said, tying the feather into Lionel's now longer hair. "I stepped away from y'all, looked up, and there it was, floating down."

Beatrice was watching when the feather floated down and noticed that her grandfather had been standing under what appeared to be a large nest.

Beatrice failed to share this observation with Lionel.

Lionel sat proudly that night at the fire feeling that now, with the feather in his hair and his bear claws, he at least *looked* like the great horsemen and like his fellow warrior Beatrice. The group saw, as they had begun to see with greater frequency, something that Mr. Hawkins called the aurora borealis; a night sky that reminded Lionel of the color-streaked morning when he had first seen the starfish.

It was on this night that Grandpa announced it was time for him to return to the Milk River, so as not to arouse the suspicions of the government.

The next morning Grandpa rode out of the meadow with a list of supplies from Mr. Hawkins, a list that included a box of yellow pencils. Grandpa promised to return soon with word and hopefully, a plan that would take them through the winter. He said that it might be time to head up to Canada, but also thought that it wasn't necessary at the moment to make a firm decision.

Lionel and Beatrice watched their grandfather disappear into the tree line, and soon a melancholy fell over the meadow. Even the usually boisterous Mr. Hawkins, who had enjoyed their grandfather's company, became withdrawn and sullen.

In the days that followed Grandpa's departure, the group continued their long walks into the Great Wood, but now walked in silence. The days of pirate adventure were traded for thoughts of what had transpired and apprehension at what still lay ahead.

It was during one of these somber forays through the trees that they became reacquainted with Tom Gunn of the Heart Butte renegades.

CHAPTER THIRTY

A BLOODIED TOM GUNN • JENKINS & LUMPKIN • "THEY'RE IN THE WOODS"

THEY WERE out hunting one day when they were startled by the sound of a large animal crashing through the undergrowth. Junebug heard it first, but Beatrice and Mr. Hawkins must have then seen it, because they both immediately broke from the group in pursuit.

Lionel, Corn Poe, and Junebug tried to follow, but soon lost Beatrice and Mr. Hawkins somewhere among the trees. They paused to catch their breath, and Junebug crouched, turning his head in owl-like fashion with every creak and groan from the big trees that surrounded them.

"What in God's creation was that?" Corn Poe gasped.

Junebug ignored him, continuing instead to rotate his head, eventually facing north, then abruptly standing and looking at Lionel. Lionel understood, and followed when Junebug suddenly broke away without making a sound.

"What—ya hear something?" Lionel heard Corn Poe call.

Lionel ran at Junebug's heels, easily weaving between the massive tree trunks that descended from the great canopy above, and jumping over the crumbling decay of logs that lay in their path.

"Come on, what did ya hear?" Corn Poe yelled from behind, struggling to catch them. "What is it?"

They ran for a long time, but did not tire. Lionel noted that with every step, the distance between them and Corn Poe's fading cries became more evident.

They ran as fast as they could until they reached a slight ridge that hung over a low depression. They paused at the lip, and below them they saw Beatrice closing in on what now appeared to be some sort of man, a thin man. The thin man ran recklessly, bouncing off trees and falling over their broken limbs. Mr. Hawkins, carrying his rifle, was right behind Beatrice.

Junebug and Lionel slid down the embankment

on a heavy blanket of leaves and scrambled to their feet in time to see Beatrice tackle the runner and disappear behind the base of a large tree. They followed as fast as they could, and in no time, rounded the tree to find Beatrice sitting on Tom Gunn, holding him facedown on the forest floor. Mr. Hawkins stood over them, collecting his breath.

"You've got to let me go, you've got to, or they're gonna catch me!" Tom Gunn spat dirt and wet rotting leaves from his mouth. "It won't take long for them to figure I'm gone!"

Beatrice stood, allowing Tom to roll over; and that's when they all saw his bruised and battered face. Tom's right eye was swollen shut, and there was a cut on his upper lip. He also wore a two-inch gash smack dab in the middle of his forehead, and his tattered turkey feathers were missing.

"I'm tellin' ya, you're best to let me go!" Tom yelled.

"Son, just take a minute to catch your breath," Mr. Hawkins said, frantically scanning the low depression where they stood.

"I just don't want 'em to catch me," Tom said, his words turning into low and heavy sobs. "I just wanna go back to school. I just wanna go home."

Lionel looked at Beatrice, who watched Tom without emotion.

"Hey, where are y'all?" suddenly boomed across the wash. "I can hear ya, but I sure the hell can't see ya."

Mr. Hawkins's head snapped in the direction of Corn Poe's voice. "That boy is just about a hair away from bein' a full-blown idiot, ain't he?"

"Come on, y'all," Corn Poe's cries continued, "where are ya?"

Mr. Hawkins shot a look at Junebug, and in a silent flash the boy was gone, running back in the direction of Corn Poe's pleading cries. Mr. Hawkins kneeled down next to Tom and helped him to sit.

"Son, you're all right now."

Lionel noticed that there was something different in Mr. Hawkins's voice and that his face had wrinkled into a concerned frown.

"Now, listen. I ain't gonna hurt ya, but I do need you to answer me this right away. How far back are these folks that did this to ya?"

Tom looked up at Mr. Hawkins with a curious expression. "They're a ways back. I've been running through the night, but they'll catch me. I know they will." Tom looked wildly around, resting his gaze on Beatrice and Lionel. "They're looking for you!"

"Me?" Corn Poe retorted, appearing from behind the big tree with Junebug at his side. "Go figure."

"Corn Poe, make yourself useful and get this boy something to drink," Mr. Hawkins instructed. Tom, although battered, bruised, and bleeding, looked to have calmed down a bit. "Now, who's after who, son? Who ya running from?" Hawkins persisted.

"The men, the government men from the outpost. They're here. They're here somewhere in the woods."

Mr. Hawkins's face tightened. Lionel watched, but Beatrice's expression remained unchanged.

"Barney decided he'd try to collect the hundred dollars for the return of the horse, but these men . . . Lumpkin and Jenkins . . . they've gone crazy. Went to hittin' me and Barney after we left the captain."

"The captain?"

"Yeah, when he heard that his horse was up in the mountains, he formed his own party to set out to retrieve 'im. Jenkins convinced the captain to let him and Lumpkin go ahead to scout. Made me and Barney go with 'em."

Corn Poe reappeared with a small flask of water and handed it to Tom, who drank it all in a single gulp.

"We were supposed to go back to where the captain is camped to report, but Jenkins, the one with the scar, he said that we're close enough and that he don't need the captain to apprehend renegade children, so he made us keep going."

"How many men's he got?" Hawkins shot, in a tone that Lionel wouldn't have recognized as his voice before today.

"Well, back at the captain's camp, they got about ten, maybe twelve, but Jenkins got about five with him, five not including Mr. Lumpkin. I left in the night 'cause Jenkins hit the bottle and went to beatin' on me and Barney, claiming we knew more than we let on and that we was leading him on what he called 'a wild goose chase.'"

Tom paused and tilted the empty flask back toward the sky, draining it of its few remaining drops.

"Barney got the worst of it. I don't think he cares for the one hundred dollars no more."

Mr. Hawkins sat back on his haunches and looked up at Junebug, who stood at the base of the tree next to Corn Poe.

"What?" Corn Poe asked.

But Mr. Hawkins stayed quiet.

CHAPTER THIRTY-ONE

BACK ON THE RUN • ELK AT THE STREAM • SWIMMING • A FIRELESS CAMP • THE TRUTH ABOUT AVERY JOHN & JUNEBUG HAWKINS

THEY RAN as a group back to the meadow in silence, Mr. Hawkins prodding Corn Poe and Tom Gunn to keep up for the majority of the journey. When they got back to the meadow Mr. Hawkins told the boys to take Tom to clean up down at the stream.

They left Mr. Hawkins and Beatrice standing in front of the lodge with the horses, and Lionel felt a heaviness that he had not experienced since they had run away from the boarding school, the same haunted presence that had left him that first night at their grandfather's house on the Milk River.

Lionel walked ahead, leaving Corn Poe rambling on to Junebug about his various theories as to the true motivations of the government's pursuit. Junebug was a good listener and therefore Corn Poe's preferred audience.

When Lionel got to the stream, from the corner of his eye he saw something move. He turned, hoping for a moment that his grandfather, having heard that there was trouble, had come back. Instead, he found that he had interrupted a family of elk drinking from the swirling stream.

Lionel watched as the elk casually drank their fill and moved from the water to the woods. Lionel locked eyes with the bull elk as he paused to show his wide antlers before fading into the trees. Lionel was still thinking about the elk's dark black eyes as Corn Poe, Tom, and Junebug reached the stream.

"My vote is that we head to Canada. They already looked for us up there, and therefore, now that they're back here, it's the last place they'll think we'll be," Corn Poe was saying as Tom lay on his belly to drink from the creek.

Lionel wondered what Beatrice would think about Corn Poe continuing to include himself in all of their plans, and now that he thought about it, he noticed that Corn Poe almost seemed to be enjoying this. He watched the other three boys and thought about Beatrice and Mr. Hawkins back at the lodge and how fast they had been able to move through the woods that very morning. How fast they had been able to move without all of them.

Lionel decided to go for a swim to clear his head and pulled off his clothes, starting with the bear claws. He hung the string of claws from a low branch of a quaking aspen, stripped off his clothes, and jumped into the stream's deepest pool. The cold water surged over Lionel's body, reviving his legs, tired from the morning's run. Lionel was happy that the tumbling waters from the stream drowned out Corn Poe, who continued to hypothesize his different plans of escape.

Lionel's head hurt, so he swam under a small waterfall and leaned forward to drink, letting the water beat onto the back of his neck and shoulders. He heard what he thought to be a distant whistle, but as he swam toward the muddy bank, realized from Junebug's reaction that it was one of Mr. Hawkins's birdcalls. He followed Corn Poe, Junebug, and Tom, gathering his piled clothes and pulling them on as he ran back to the lodge.

Mr. Hawkins stood before the lodge, cinching the saddles on his already loaded horses. He worked quickly, barely acknowledging the boys as they ran across the meadow to join him. Lionel looked around for Beatrice and Ulysses.

"I must be outta my head. I should just be takin' my boy and leavin' the rest of ya," Mr. Hawkins said, more to himself than to the rest of them. "Me and old Junebug got ourselves organized and know how to move. I can't say the same about the rest of you."

Mr. Hawkins lifted a heavy sack of flour onto the back of one of the packhorses and tied the thick canvas over it.

"And you," Hawkins said, turning to Corn Poe, "I don't want no more foolishness. No more of this idle chatter. You're to keep your mouth shut and do what you're told! I want you to think before ya speak."

Beatrice appeared from behind the lodge, riding high on Ulysses's back. Their few supplies were already tied in small bundles to the great horse's neck.

"Do ya hear me, boy?" Mr. Hawkins demanded. "'Cause I'll leave ya here, if not. I'll leave ya right here!"

Corn Poe stood, surprisingly speechless.

"Now, gather your things. You do the same, Lionel. Check to see if your sister got everything."

Lionel and Corn Poe ran into the lodge, fueled by the urgency in Mr. Hawkins's voice. Avery John Hawkins seemed like a different person, the anger making his voice almost unrecognizable.

They crossed the crooked doorframe and Lionel paused, impatiently letting his eyes adjust to the dim light. As the cavernous fireplace slowly came into view, Lionel wondered if this was the last time he would ever see the lodge. Corn Poe scrambled about, blindly throwing his only other shirt, his spare pair of woolen socks, and a blue tin cup into his heavy jacket.

"That's my kit," he said, and shot back out the door.

Lionel surveyed the room once more. His sister had, while he was swimming, taken care of everything.

They rode for the rest of the day and into the night. They rode higher and higher up into the mountains, Beatrice and Lionel on the back of Ulysses, Junebug and Mr. Hawkins on their horses, and Corn Poe and Tom Gunn riding on the pack horses that

Mr. Hawkins led up the winding, narrow trail. Lionel could see the meadow and the lodge spiraling farther and farther below them as they climbed higher and higher. He wondered—if their grandfather did return, how would he find them? He wondered where Mr. Hawkins was taking them.

That night they made a small camp, but Mr. Hawkins warned them not to get comfortable, as they would be moving out long before the first light of morning. He wouldn't let them start a fire as it could give away their position, but instead stood over them, unpacking a portion of their load, continuing to go on about Corn Poe and his particular ability to create mischief.

"We should never have stopped," Mr. Hawkins went on, mumbling to himself. "As much as I love that little lodge in the summers, we should'a kept going the second we saw the smoke rising from that crumbled and crooked ol' chimney. Nine times outta ten, these days, where there's smoke, there's people; and where there's people, there's problems. And now, oh now, we got the lion's share in all of 'em."

Mr. Hawkins threw his saddle to the ground and flung himself into an unhappy heap against it. The children gathered in a small circle around a fire that wasn't there and sat, eating the stringy smoked meat.

The moon rose, accompanied by the ever present sounds of the night. Lionel knew that the steady creak and moan of the trees, the swelling cacophony of crickets, and the intermittent calls from the night owls had been there all along; but now as they sat without speaking, the nocturnal cries took the forefront, and lay over the already heavy weight of this particular evening.

Lionel was looking up at the stars when Corn Poe spoke.

"Excuse me, Mr. Hawkins. I don't mean to intrude or wake ya if you're sleepin'," he said, just a notch above a whisper.

"I ain't sleepin'," Hawkins responded, lying on his side with his head turned to the night.

"If you don't mind me askin' ya somethin'. Somethin' of a personal nature?" Corn Poe continued.

Mr. Hawkins rolled over, looking more curious than disturbed. "I suppose it would depend on the nature of the question, and if I was you, I'd think long and hard about what you're askin'."

Corn Poe sat quietly for a moment and then continued, "Well, I suppose in one sense it ain't none of my business. But, on the other, it truly is. Ya see, I figure that now that we're travelin' with each other, I got a right to know on account it may have some influence on me and my well-being and that of my friends."

"Well, this ought to be one helluva question," Mr. Hawkins said, sitting up and gazing across the patch of moonlight toward the children. "Well, then, go ahead. I'll do my best to answer if I choose to."

Lionel studied Corn Poe's expression. He always looked a little uneasy, so it was hard to tell if there was any sort of change in his demeanor. Tom Gunn sat next to him, staring at his feet.

Corn Poe continued, "Well, what it is I'm wonderin' is how come you and Junebug here are on the run? I mean, Lionel and Beatrice is runnin' on account of bein' horse thieves. I suppose I fell in with 'em, so that puts me as an accessory to the crime. But what about you? What about the Junebug? Why y'all out here? Why y'all so hell bent on runnin'?"

Lionel looked at Junebug, and then at Beatrice and Tom Gunn. Lionel had never thought to ask and doubted if he had ever wondered why Mr. Hawkins and Junebug chose to live in the mountains. Lionel just assumed that this was where they lived. He wondered if Beatrice knew. He wondered if she cared.

"I suppose I can tell ya, as it may have a bearing on how this all unfolds. Hell, maybe it'll sway ya to decide it's time to part company, and we can move on guilt-free," Hawkins said with a distant look in his eye. He leaned forward and stared at Corn Poe with a blank expression on his face.

"I killed a man—two men—with my bare hands. I'd killed men before, but then it was all right. It's all right to a kill a man as long as the government tells ya to kill 'im. But in this case, I did it on my own; and now they're dead, the both of 'em, dead."

Corn Poe's face lit up, but he fought to control himself and spoke again in the same hushed tone with which he had started the conversation. "Well, if'n you did, you must'a had your reasons."

Mr. Hawkins looked over at Junebug and then to the harvest moon that hung like a rotting pumpkin over the treetops. "They came after my missus and the boy there. She was dead when I found them and now, so are they. That's all ya need to know. Ya understand me? That's all ya need to know."

"Yes, sir. I understand," Corn Poe said, looking both satisfied with the answer and relieved that he had asked the question that had been on his mind.

"I suggest ya put that outta your head. It's in the past," Mr. Hawkins said, lying back into his saddle. "Now, you get some sleep."

Lionel lay back on the buffalo robe. His legs were tired, and his head still hurt. He tried to put it out of his mind, but he couldn't help but think about Mr. Hawkins killing the men, and wondered if he felt bad about what had happened. He remembered that Beatrice had told their grandfather that she hadn't felt bad when she drove the sheep shears into Jenkins's hand, but Lionel wondered if this was different. Lionel knew that Sergeant Jenkins had deserved it, but those men, the men that Mr. Hawkins was talking about, weren't stabbed in the hand, they were dead. But they were dead because they killed Mr. Hawkins's wife, Junebug's mother. Lionel closed his eyes, hoping that tomorrow would be a better day for all of them.

Soon, Lionel fell into a deep sleep and dreamed once again of the Frozen Man. He stood in a grove of quaking aspen with the Frozen Man, staring out across the grass sea. He saw Beatrice and his grandfather on their raft, sailing east away from the shore, away from him. He also saw a small ship, and on this ship he saw Mr. Hawkins, Junebug, and all their horses. Lionel turned away from the lake toward the woods. Corn Poe was riding through the trees on Ulysses. Lionel looked back to the Frozen Man and noticed for the first time that the Frozen Man, not Lionel, was wearing the string of bear claws around his frosted neck.

Lionel sat up with a start, clutching at his neck for the bear claws. They weren't there. He looked around in the darkness. It was raining, and Lionel wasn't in a grove of aspen with the Frozen Man. He was wrapped in the buffalo robe in the mountains above the lodge in the meadow. Mr. Hawkins was crouched, tying the last corner of a tarp over Lionel's head. The rain thundered on the tarp, but now they were all dry, or as dry as could be expected.

"Go back to sleep there, Lionel," Mr. Hawkins whispered. "It's all right, just a little rain."

Lionel watched Mr. Hawkins's silhouette as he settled back down against his saddle. "Just a little rain."

Lionel felt around the buffalo robe to see if the claws had come off while he was sleeping. They weren't there. Had someone taken them? He looked around suspiciously. Who would take them? Then he thought about all that had happened that day and remembered that the last time he had seen the bear claws had been when he went swimming down by the stream. He had left them. He had left the string of bear claws by the stream in the meadow.

Not knowing what to do, he considered waking Beatrice and telling her, to see what she thought, but he could hear her heavy breathing and knew that it was rare that he was awake at a time when she wasn't. He had often wondered if she ever slept.

For a moment he lay listening to the rain splatter on the tarp. He had to go back. He had to go back to get the bear claws.

Chapter Thirty-Two

Running in the Rain • A Talking Wolverine • The Pirate's Tree • The Colliding Mule • Mr. Hawkins

Lionel waited until everyone's breathing turned heavy, and then, when it did, continued to wait, wanting to make certain that he did not wake any of them, especially Mr. Hawkins.

Finally, Lionel folded back the buffalo robe and crawled out from under the tarp and into the rainy, black night. Hunched low, he sprinted from their encampment back to the trail that their caravan cut in their escape from the meadow.

He ran as best he could back down the spiraling path. Small rivers poured down the center of the game trail, and twice Lionel fell as he made his way to the valley below. He ran until he could run no farther, then assured himself that there was still plenty of night and that he would be back with the bear claws before morning and that none of them would know he had ever left.

The trail dropped down into the valley, and although it took longer than he had hoped, Lionel soon found himself running once again, this time parallel to the stream that would eventually lead him back to the meadow. Lionel looked to the east, where the morning would soon show itself in the distant clouded skies.

Lionel slowed once he reached the small grove of aspen, keeping an eye out for the branch where he had hung the claws. It had stopped raining, and as the clouds cleared, with the first hint of the new day, Lionel realized that he had wandered past their swimming hole. He thought that he had perhaps overshot that entire part of the river. He made his way back along the bank and once again found himself in a tight thicket of aspen, the same aspen from his dream. Lionel wandered through the maze, unable to get his bearings. He knew he was close, so how could he miss it? Lionel stood, scared and unsure as to what he should do next. He thought about giving up and heading back to find Beatrice and Mr. Hawkins and the others; but then something shiny fell from the sky.

Lionel moved a few paces into the small grove to investigate and found a shiny gold button in the rotting leaves that covered the forest floor. He picked it up and noticed that it had an eagle engraved on it, similar to the military buttons on the coat that the captain had given him. He ran a finger down his jacket's open flap and was surprised to find that they were all still firmly intact. A dark shadow passed over him, and Lionel looked up to see the fleeting tail feathers of the raven from their meadow.

The raven zigzagged from tree to tree, surveying the stream in the clear morning light. Lionel remembered the raven's pulling buttons from the straw man's silk dress. He put this dropped button in his pocket and followed the bird, hoping that it was on its way back to and not away from the meadow. He found himself running to keep up and in no time he stood breathless at the familiar rise that led to the small pool with the waterfall. He climbed the rise, and there, hanging on the slim branch in a tight clump of quaking aspen, was the string of bear claws, exactly where he had left them. Lionel looked to the treetops to thank the bird, but the raven was gone.

Lionel climbed the rise and took the claws from the branch. The leather that held them was wet, but all seemed to be intact. He tied the bear claws around his neck and then dropped to the bank to drink from the cold swirling waters.

When he'd had enough, Lionel rolled over onto his back. He caught his breath, feeling relieved to have recovered the Frozen Man's gift, and wondering how the raven had happened upon the button that was now in his pocket. Lionel knew that he should immediately turn back and run as fast as he could to rejoin the others, but thought that while he was catching his breath, it wouldn't hurt to have another look at the lodge that had been their home.

He scrambled to his feet and dropped down into the meadow. Their garden held the last of the season's offerings, but in the pale light of morning it looked lonely and overgrown with all that had transpired over the last couple of days. Lionel looked at the slumped straw man and thought about the day that his grandfather had sat on the stool weaving it to life; the same stool that Corn Poe had threatened to crack across Mr. Hawkins's head.

Lionel wandered a bit farther out into the meadow, thinking about Mr. Hawkins and wondering what his life would have been like if those men hadn't killed his wife. He wondered if Mr. Hawkins, his wife, and Junebug might have liked to live in the little lodge year-round. Lionel thought that he and Beatrice would have, but not anymore. They were back on the run—but where would they run to now?

A commotion from the stream below startled him. He whipped around to see the big, black-eyed elk burst from behind the garden and bolt across a section of the meadow toward the cover of the Great Wood. The big elk ran toward the tree line, but then, almost as a second thought, changed direction and ran directly toward the lodge, continuing to the trees that stood behind it and the smokehouse.

Lionel dropped into a crouching position, hiding in the high grass of the meadow, and stared back toward the stream. Something had startled the elk, and there, back in the trees, he saw what it was. Men—government men on horseback, and some on foot.

Heart pounding, Lionel spun around and hurried toward the shelter of the Great Wood, but then, like the elk, changed direction and broke toward the lodge. There were more men back in the trees.

He ran toward the lodge, throwing himself against the crooked door, and tumbling into his former home. He rolled to the window and carefully stole a look toward the stream.

The men on horseback appeared on the rise and entered the small meadow. Lionel craned his neck toward the Great Wood where he saw more men appear. He dropped from the window and leaned against the lodge's rough-hewn logs. His heart was racing, and he could hear his own labored breathing. He slowly rose up for another look.

Some of the men had dismounted, and their horses had wandered into the recently neglected garden, helping themselves to the remnants. Lionel thought he caught a glimpse of Brother Finn and the captain himself, but dropped back down before he could be sure. Lionel looked around the lodge, trying to think of what his grandfather would do. He decided to take one more look outside and see if there was a way he could make it to the Great Wood. If he could make it to the woods, he could find his way around the meadow and back up to the trail to rejoin Beatrice and Mr. Hawkins.

Peering through the window, Lionel thought he saw a soldier lowering Barney Little Plume from the back of a horse to the ground. Barney's hands looked as though they were tied behind his back. Lionel looked back toward the stream and the garden. An assemblage of soldiers was now heading directly toward the lodge.

Lionel fell to the floor on the verge of tears. He was trapped. He thought about Beatrice and his grandfather and wondered again what they would do. Beatrice wouldn't have to do anything, because she wouldn't have gotten herself into this situation. Beatrice wouldn't have left the bear claws in the first place, let alone taken the time to go swimming in light of all that had happened. And if she had forgotten them, upon return, she would have grabbed the string of claws and left. She wouldn't have waited around to be joined by these men.

Lionel thought about his grandfather. Once again, the only conclusion that Lionel could come to was that his grandfather wouldn't be in this situation. He would have been more careful with the claws. Lionel had learned so much since he had left school—but what of it could he use now?

He buried his head between his knees and shoved his hands deep into his pockets. He felt the gold button that the raven had dropped . . . then he thought of the elk . . . the elk . . .

Be aware of what's around you and watch. Listen to the animals, the wind, the mountains.

His grandfather was right. The raven and the elk in their own ways had just warned him. They had told him that there were men in the woods.

Grandpa's words ran through his head. His eyes darted anxiously around the abandoned lodge, finally resting on the slumping chimney. His hand shot down to the raised scar on his leg. The wolverine. Lionel looked once more out the window. The soldiers were almost to the lodge. He dropped back down and scrambled on all fours toward the chimney and the crack—the same crack they figured the wolverine had crawled through. Depending on where you stood in the room, you might not even notice the crevice, let alone think that something—or someone—could actually fit there.

Lionel climbed up onto the chimney and then pulled himself into the wolverine's passage. Just as he disappeared into the damp, musty space, he heard the men kick in the lodge's crooked door, followed by the sound of smashing glass. Lionel could see the soldiers in slivers of glimpses between the crumbled rocks.

"Would you take a look at this dump?" one of the soldiers snarled. Lionel knew that voice; it washed over him like a nightmare. It was Jenkins, Sergeant Haskell Jenkins.

Lionel saw the sneering grin and coarse black patch as Jenkins flashed across the chimney's fissure. There he was, smashing and breaking his way across their lodge.

Lionel's fear turned to anger. He wanted to attack Jenkins where he stood for what he had tried to do to his sister, but thought better of it. Lionel knew he had to get out of there. He had to find and warn Beatrice. He had to warn Mr. Hawkins, Junebug, Corn Poe, and even Tom Gunn.

"Jenkins, Sergeant Jenkins." Lionel heard a familiar voice entering the lodge. He looked toward the door and saw that it was the captain who addressed Jenkins, and he did not sound happy.

"What on earth is that boy doing bound, Sergeant Jenkins?" the captain demanded, hooking his thumb to the yard where Barney now stood under guard.

"I consider him a hostile, sir," Jenkins answered.

"A hostile?" the captain responded in disbelief. "That's preposterous. He's only a boy."

"There were plenty of 'boys' who went hostile during the campaign," Jenkins said in a rather matter-of-fact tone.

"The campaign is over. It has been for some time. As a matter of fact, Sergeant, I can't quite recall your being there." The captain turned to the other soldiers who stood in the doorframe. "I want that boy released immediately. And see to it that he's cleaned up and fed."

The other soldiers scurried, leaving Jenkins and the captain alone in the lodge.

"And where have you been, Sergeant? You were supposed to scout ahead and return to report to me. That was over two days ago," the captain growled.

"Why, we were right on their trail, sir. I thought it best under the circumstances to continue the pursuit. If I hadn't been forced back to meet ya here, I'd bet my last silver dollar I'd have them horse thieves in custody already."

"That is not the issue," the captain shot back.

"You were under orders, and I'd be within my rights to relieve you of your duties."

Lionel watched the captain circle the room. He looked older. He looked tired.

"I want a full report when we return to the post," the captain continued. "Your conduct is suspect and highly unorthodox."

"Aye, Captain, as unorthodox as it may be, I've been charged with the return of stolen property and the apprehension of horse thieves, and that is what I intend to do."

"That you were," the captain countered, "but you will do so under my command and in a manner befitting a solider. Is that understood, Sergeant?"

Jenkins spat on the floor and moved toward the door.

"Sergeant, is that understood?"

"Aye, Captain. Clear as crystal. Now, sir, beggin' the captain's pardon, I'd like to continue the search. I believe them perpetrators to be in the immediate vicinity."

Jenkins gave the captain a halfhearted salute and then left. Lionel sat silently watching as the captain returned the salute to no one, and then continued to examine the lodge. He wandered over to the chimney and stood dangerously close to where Lionel was hiding.

Lionel wondered if he should reveal himself and try to explain to the captain what had happened and why he had taken Ulysses. Lionel liked the captain and was sure that he missed the big horse. He wanted to let the captain know that he had continued to care for the horse in his absence.

But the captain turned and walked abruptly out the door, leaving Lionel to consider making a run for it and trying to lose the men in a break for the Great Wood. This seemed unlikely, as the voices of the soldiers had spread out from one side of the meadow to the other. Lionel could hear Jenkins's voice above all of the others as he barked orders urging his men to prepare to continue their mission of returning the captain's horse and apprehending those responsible for its theft.

There had to be another way. Lionel ran his hands down the contours of the chimney's piled river rocks and felt tufts of hair from the wolverine among the cobwebs and dust. There was a steady flow of air on his wet moccasins, so he crouched down on his knees to try to get his head in a position to investigate. He felt the air streaming with greater force and realized that the crack in the chimney continued to the exterior of the lodge. Lionel contorted his body, twisting himself to where he was practically standing on his head. He could see a small ray of light from outside and decided that he had to get out of the chimney so he could run back to warn the others.

Lionel moved further into the crevice and inched himself toward the light. The space was cramped, but he pulled himself along on his belly, quietly moving small piles of debris as he went. He sensed movement above him as he crawled, and when he reached the light of the small opening, he stopped.

The rock above seemed to be alive, moving almost as if it were breathing. Lionel's eyes adjusted to the light and he realized that it wasn't the chimney that was moving but a swarm of daddy longlegs dangling in a tight bunch just inches above his head. Lionel wasn't afraid of spiders, but this was a lot of them. He quickly moved forward until he was in a position to push his head out the crevice at the back of the chimney and make a break for the tree line that stood ten paces from where he was hiding.

Lionel could see the soldiers readying themselves from his new hiding place. He tried to get a count for Mr. Hawkins, but with all the movement and his limited view, he had trouble keeping track of the men. He thought that there must have been at least twelve, but that there could be as many as twenty. All this in pursuit of Beatrice, Lionel, and Ulysses; Lionel figured that the captain must really miss his horse.

He crawled out as far as he dared and eyed a break in the trees. He took another look at the soldiers and saw that Brother Finn was bringing Barney up from the stream. Barney's clothes were torn and bloody, and his face was battered, cut, and bruised, just like Tom Gunn's. Lionel didn't feel particularly friendly toward Barney—or Tom Gunn, for that matter. After all, they had been the ones who had joined up with the government to collect money at his and Beatrice's expense. But he still felt sorry for them. Barney looked scared despite now being untied, and Lionel noticed that he stuck as close as he could to Brother Finn's and the captain's sides.

Lionel looked back toward the woods and decided that it was now or never—he had to make a break for it. He pulled himself forward out of the hole and into the high grass that stretched up the back side of the exterior chimney. There, out of the corner of his eye, Lionel saw a soldier coming toward him. He felt a leaping in his throat. This wasn't just any soldier. It was Jenkins's buddy from the water trough, Private Samuel Lumpkin.

He thought about pulling himself back into the safety of the chimney, but a moment later, without thinking, sprang to his feet and ran to the trees. Lionel heard a rough, grumbled burst of surprise from Lumpkin as he ran across the open section of the meadow. Lionel looked over his shoulder as he burst into the shade of the wood to see Lumpkin raise his rifle and aim toward the thick foliage. He aimed it at Lionel.

"Stop!" Private Lumpkin yelled, but Lionel kept running.

Lionel heard the first bullet whiz wildly over his head, followed by the echoing crack of the rifle. Lumpkin fired again, prompting shots from other soldiers, but Lionel kept running. In the distance, he could hear the captain calling for the men to stop firing, but another volley hurtled past him and he watched the bullets bite into the soft bark flesh of the trees that stood before him.

Lionel continued to run. He could hear the men enter the woods behind him and then heard men on horses. The horsemen had trouble following Lionel directly as he ran, jumped, slid, and climbed his way across the Great Wood, but he couldn't shake them. He dropped, stumbling down into a gully, and then scrambled up the other side. He saw the men drop into the gully, so he quickly changed direction by climbing up the exposed roots of a toppled tree and running the length of its fallen torso toward its upper branches.

As Lionel ran, he realized where he was. This trunk was once the deck of his ship, the branches its rigging and mast. He was in the stretch of broken trees where they had played pirate, and he knew this terrain well. He stopped and looked around the wood and thought about the long days of summer when they had played out Mr. Hawkins's pirate tales in these tangles. Now he was also running, but instead of in search of make-believe buried treasure or evading imaginary captors, he ran for his life.

Lionel climbed through the thicket of branches at the tree's prone top and then jumped down to another trunk that lay rotting underneath. He heard the men coming out of the wash and dropped to the far side of this tree, and burrowed himself under the trap of leaves collected at the elongated base.

Lionel lay, trying to slow his heavy breathing. He thought that his heart was about to burst out of his chest, and he could hear the men's horses approach the clutter of fallen trees and stop.

"I've lost his trail, Sergeant," a soldier reported. "It just disappeared."

"Well, find it!" Lionel heard Jenkins shout.

Lionel held his breath and exhaled slowly through his nose as more men entered the area.

"Spread out—he can't have gone far!" Jenkins continued to bellow as another horseman joined him just on the other side of Lionel's hiding place.

"What do you make of it?" It was Private Lumpkin.

"What do I make of it?" Jenkins shot back. "I think that the captain's gone soft is what I make of it! Back in the day, if ya didn't hang rustlers ya would, at the very least, have 'em horsewhipped! Soft, I tell ya! Soft!"

Lionel lay under the rotting earth listening to Lumpkin and Jenkins continue to commiserate.

"Ya give these bastards an inch . . ." But Jenkins was interrupted as "Over here—I've found tracks!" echoed through the woods.

"This best be him," Jenkins said, jerking his horse's head, and then he and Private Lumpkin were gone.

Lionel could hear the men as they moved to where the calls continued. Boy, had he done it this time, he thought, feeling the heavy ring of bear claws around his neck. How was he supposed to find Beatrice without leading these men straight to her?

He pushed the wet leaves off him and slowly raised his head. He thought about cutting directly across the Great Wood to the base of the mountains. Maybe he could forgo the switchback trail and just climb straight up to where he had last seen Beatrice, Mr. Hawkins, and the rest of them?

He climbed over the trunk and, keeping low to the ground, cut across the woods back toward the meadow. He could hear Jenkins calling out orders and thought at one point that his scar-snarled voice grew louder as though he was, once again, getting closer.

Lionel ran as fast as he could, but the soldiers

seemed to be multiplying among the trees that towered above them all. Lionel thought about how over the course of this summer, he and his sister had spoken in reverent whispers in these woods. These soldiers could be heard clear to Canada, if anyone was listening.

He ran down another wash and fell as he tried to make his way up the other side. His legs ached, and his lungs felt as though they were on fire; but the voices and the sound of approaching hooves made him get back on his feet. Lionel wondered if he should try to hide again or make a final, desperate break for the meadow.

Something moved somewhere above him, and Lionel ran. He came out of the lower end of the depression and turned to find Jenkins riding at breakneck speed directly toward him. Lionel spun around and ran, the heavy breathing of Jenkins's horse getting closer with every beat of Lionel's thundering heart.

"There he is! Over here!" bounced from tree to tree.

Lionel could hear the horse at his heels and knew that it was only a matter of seconds before Jenkins was on top of him. He felt a biting sting slash across his back and shoulder, and fell. He looked up to see Jenkins turning his horse, a riding whip still swinging from his wrist.

"You stay put and quit all this runnin' and carryin' on!" Jenkins growled, raising the whip high above his head and bringing it back down on Lionel as he lay in a heap on the forest floor.

Lionel felt the burn of the whip. He covered his head with his hands as another blow landed, then looked up through clenched fingers to see a streaking shadow pass directly in front of him and collide with Jenkins's horse. Jenkins flew from his saddle, and his horse fell, barely missing him.

Lionel looked up to see Beatrice turn Ulysses on a dime. She was holding their grandfather's rifle in one hand, the rawhide reins in the other. Her face was once again painted in the dark black mask that she had worn at the sweat lodge with Barney and Tom Gunn. She looked wild, like a creature of these woods, as she drove her heels harder into Ulysses's side.

Jenkins pulled a large pistol from its holster as he stumbled to his feet. Beatrice and Ulysses countered, making another pass; this time Beatrice brought the butt of their grandfather's rifle across the side of Jenkins's head.

More soldiers emerged from the trees, and Lionel thought he heard shots fired. Before he knew it, he was running again; now somewhat frightened by the fierce intensity that showed in Beatrice's blackened eyes.

Beatrice pulled Ulysses around to make another pass at Jenkins, but then, seeing the approaching men, thought better of it and spurred the big horse toward Lionel. The men fired their rifles despite the captain's orders, so Lionel kept running, oblivious to the fact that Beatrice was behind him. The next thing Lionel knew, Beatrice had swooped him up into her arms and set him in front of her, straddling Ulysses's withers. She pushed Lionel's head down and drove the horse harder through the trees.

Lionel looked up trying to catch his breath. He couldn't get more than a sip of air into his burning lungs. He saw flashes through the trees of government horsemen trying to get ahead of Ulysses and cut off their escape. Now, Lionel thought, we'll see how fast Ulysses really is. Ulysses must have somehow heard what Lionel was thinking, because the big horse dug in and sped ahead of the men. Tree branches slapped at them as they outstripped the pursuing government horsemen.

Lionel looked back and saw that more horsemen had quickly joined them, and that one of them was Jenkins. Jenkins rode, beating his horse forward with unrelenting fury despite the steady stream of blood that poured down the creviced scar on his face.

"Beatrice!" Lionel cried. "They're coming!"

Ulysses answered for her, putting more ground between the children and the soldiers. Lionel wrapped his arms around Ulysses's neck and lowered his head further. He could see an opening in the trees ahead and thought that they must have reached the end of the Great Wood. He looked to his right and saw another cluster of horsemen slashing across the trees in front of them.

Beatrice must have seen them too, because she pulled the big horse farther toward the opening in the trees; but one of the men cut with them, and as they reached the clearing, the two horses were running neck and neck. The government rider was just about on top of them when Lionel saw yet another horseman break from the tree line.

Lionel hung on for his life. The government rider was so close, Lionel could almost touch him. The rider pulled even closer and reached out to grab ahold of Ulysses's reins; but Beatrice batted his arm away with the rifle.

The rider tried again, but then their grandfather suddenly appeared at the man's side. Lionel could not believe his eyes. His grandfather was riding his mule on a direct collision course.

Beatrice spurred the big horse forward just as their grandfather sandwiched the government rider between his mule and Ulysses's right flank. Beatrice and Lionel turned to see their grandfather reach up and effortlessly knock the man off the back of his horse. Lionel felt like cheering but knew that they were a long way from safety.

They rode fast, now side by side with their grandfather as they crossed the clearing toward a strange rock outcropping that was cluttered with fallen timber. Lionel looked back and saw that Jenkins had reached the opposite tree line.

Jenkins dismounted and was raising his rifle to shoot.

Ulysses continued running, the trees that lined

the clearing passing in a blur on either side. Lionel looked back just after Jenkins fired and heard the shot spiral overhead. Beatrice turned Ulysses toward a large fallen tree that even on its side looked to be about ten feet high. Another shot rang overhead, and Lionel saw Mr. Hawkins appear crouched on the top of a log straight ahead of them.

Mr. Hawkins leveled his heavy rifle on the rot of the fallen log and fired twice, both shots hurtling past Lionel, Beatrice, and their grandfather, then splintering a tree branch on the opposite end of the clearing just above Jenkins's head.

"Now, I missed them first two on purpose! The next time I pull this trigger you best believe it's gonna be different!" Hawkins shouted, the delayed thunder of his rifle rolling in echoes across the woods as if to emphasize his point.

Jenkins and the rest of the government men bolted for cover, and an eerie calm fell over the clearing. Ulysses continued into the safety of a cluster of rocks across the far end of the clearing opposite from Mr. Hawkins's position. When they rounded the corner, Lionel was surprised to see Corn Poe and Tom Gunn hunkered down with their hands over their heads.

"They're shootin' at us!" Corn Poe exclaimed as though some of their party hadn't figured it out yet.

Beatrice didn't bother spending time alleviating Corn Poe's concerns or commenting on his obvious claim. Before Ulysses even stopped, she dropped off the horse, and with their grandfather's rifle in hand, scrambled up to the high point of the rocks.

Lionel could see Junebug lying on his back about fifty paces away from them behind the big fallen log, holding the Hawkins's string of horses by the reins. Mr. Hawkins remained against the trunk with the heavy rifle sighted and aimed in the direction where Lionel had last seen Jenkins.

Mr. Hawkins turned, and with a wild look in his eye, shouted across their end of the clearing, "Y'all all right? They didn't hurt ya, did they?"

Their grandfather waved as Lionel dropped from Ulysses's back and into his arms.

"You okay, boy?" their grandfather said, looking over the welts from Jenkins's whip.

Lionel answered by burying his head into his grandfather's chest as random shots from the government's guns continued to crack and whiz into and off of the rocks surrounding them.

"Now, just where in the hell did you get to?" was all Corn Poe could think to say.

When Lionel looked up to answer, he realized it was too late. Jenkins and the government men were on top of them.

CHAPTER THIRTY-THREE

HUNKERED DOWN • JENKINS'S HANDS AND HAWKINS'S ACCORD

JENKINS REACHED them first. He and Lumpkin had dismounted and continued on foot through the trees that skirted the clearing to the huddled rocks where they hid. Jenkins appeared from their blind side, and before anyone knew it, knocked their grandfather to the ground and turned, facing Ulysses and Lionel.

"I told ya to quit yer runnin'," Jenkins said through clenched teeth. "Now ya gone and really made yerself some troubles."

Jenkins inched forward as more soldiers emerged from the trees.

"Now, hand me the reins to that goddamned horse before I cut ya from guts to gullet," he said, pulling the Frozen Man's knife from his army belt.

Lionel noticed for the first time that a single bear claw curled around the hilt of the Frozen Man's long, jagged blade. He looked from the knife to his grandfather, who, although back on his feet, stood staring into the barrel of Lumpkin's rifle.

"Ya leave that boy alone," Grandpa demanded. "This is a matter for the captain."

"Well, the captain ain't quite here, is he?" Jenkins said, inching closer. "And I've got a little score to settle with yer sister, don't I, Li-o-nel? It *is* Li-o-nel ain't it?"

Lionel looked down at the shiny, taut skin stretched and sutured across the back of Jenkins's hand.

"Ya lookin' at me hand, ain't ya? You remember, huh? Yer sister Beatrice is quite handy with the shears when she wants to be. But don't you worry; while it ain't what I'd call operatin' at one hundred percent, the doctors did patch 'er up, and she works just fine."

Jenkins clenched the mangle of tight sinew into a fist to emphasize his point.

"Now, I've grown tired of askin' . . . where's yer sister?"

Beatrice did not allow Lionel to answer. She

jumped from the rocks above and knocked Jenkins, once again, to the ground. Jenkins dropped the Frozen Man's knife, and in a split second Beatrice held it with both hands high above her head. Jenkins clamored for his pistol, but never reached it. Lionel watched as Beatrice drove the blade down as hard as she could, pinning Jenkins's good hand to the earth where he lay.

They all stood for a silent moment before Jenkins let out the first of many bloodcurdling screams. Lumpkin spun around and cracked Beatrice in the ribs as hard as he could with his rifle. She fell against the rock as he threw back the lever to take aim.

"Kill her!" Jenkins screamed. "Kill her!"

Grandpa was reaching out toward Lumpkin when a shot was fired, but it wasn't from Lumpkin's gun.

"You pull that trigger and I'll blow ya to kingdom come!" suddenly boomed across the clearing from tree line to tree line.

Lionel turned to see Mr. Hawkins and Junebug, now on horseback, with both of their rifles trained on Lumpkin's head. A small spiral of blue smoke drifted from the barrel of Mr. Hawkins's rifle.

"I've had just about enough of this!" Hawkins

declared, a slight tremble in his voice. "You drop that rifle, or I swear to God, damn the consequences, I will shoot you dead where you stand."

Lumpkin stole a hesitant glance at Jenkins.

"I mean it!" Mr. Hawkins shouted, firing the rifle again in the air.

Lumpkin lowered his rifle as more of the government men, including the captain, entered the clearing.

"That goes for all of y'all!" Hawkins shouted, turning toward the captain. "Me and the boy will keep pullin' these here triggers until we can't pull 'em no more!"

Lionel looked at Mr. Hawkins. His eyes were bright with fear and rage.

"The fact there's more of y'all don't matter to me." The barrel of Mr. Hawkins's rifle was now pointing directly at the captain. "If it comes to it, and you're set on gunning us down, you better think about which ones me and the boy end up taking with us. I promise, it will be a fair percentage!"

The captain lowered his pistol and stepped his horse forward. "I don't think it needs to come to that."

"I sure in hell hope it don't! I don't like killin' folk, but if it's between me or them, I will if I have to!" Hawkins returned.

"I assure you, if you please lower the rifle, I'll see that this is all dealt with justly."

"Don't do it, Captain!" Jenkins spat, clutching his bloody hand with the mutilated one. "That there is Avery John Hawkins. He's a wanted man. A murderer. I've seen the warrant for his arrest. Figures we'd find him in cahoots with this lot."

The captain turned to Hawkins, the pistol lower, but still in hand.

"Yes, sir. I am a wanted man, but don't make the mistake of thinkin' that you're bringin' me in today," Hawkins shouted, the heavy rifle balanced now between Jenkins, Lumpkin, and the captain.

Lionel thought that during these few fleeting moments, the earth must have slowed down just a bit. All of the men who now stood, guns aimed at each other, were silent. He could hear the wind in the tops of the trees, the unsettled, subtle movements of the horses, and what he thought must have been the rapid beat of his own heart. But the moment didn't last.

"I'll tell ya what I'll do. I'll make a deal with ya,"

Mr. Hawkins continued. "If you promise me that you'll see to it that these children is treated fairly, I'll let as many of your men as I could have killed live."

The government men shifted uneasily.

"Me and the boy, we just want to be left alone, so we're gonna go. You can follow if ya like, but that's the deal. I'll let ya live right now, if you do the same."

The captain looked to Beatrice and Lionel's grandfather. Everyone else's eyes darted anxiously from the captain to Mr. Hawkins.

"That's the deal, and the only way there ain't gonna be further bloodshed."

"Okay, Hawkins, deal," the captain said. "You have today."

"Soft, I tell ya!" Jenkins cried.

"And, Corporal," the captain said to one of his soldiers, "place Sergeant Jenkins and Private Lumpkin under arrest."

"Under arrest?" Jenkins sputtered.

"I warned you! Now, don't worsen your situation!" the captain shouted, silencing Jenkins instantly. The captain turned his horse to face Hawkins. "Do we have an agreement?"

"We do," Hawkins answered, his rifle still pointed

at the soldiers. He looked over at Beatrice, who lay at Lumpkin's feet. "I'm sorry, Beatrice . . . Lionel. You couldn't come where me and the Junebug are going, anyhow."

"What about me?" Corn Poe exclaimed.

Mr. Hawkins looked at the boy.

"It's best for you to stay, Corn Poe. You stay with Lionel, there. He'll take care of ya, won't ya, Lionel?"

Lionel looked up at Mr. Hawkins on his big horse and then over to Junebug sitting silently next to him.

"You all gonna be all right," Mr. Hawkins said, with a hint of question to it.

"We're all right," their grandfather answered, pulling a box of yellow pencils from his coat pocket. "We'll be just fine."

Grandpa tossed the box to Junebug, releasing the Hawkinses after all they had done for Lionel and Beatrice. Junebug caught the box, nodded, and the Hawkinses turned their horses, rifles still at the ready, and a moment later, they were gone.

CHAPTER THIRTY-FOUR

A COLD, WET RAIN • BACK TO THE LODGE • THE CAPTAIN • BEATRICE

THE CAPTAIN ordered the soldiers to give them water and food and to attend to the crack in Beatrice's ribs from Lumpkin's rifle. They sat, soldiers and Blackfeet alike, mulling over the events that led them all to be huddled at this far edge of the Great Wood.

Jenkins and Lumpkin were untied but under guard, and sat in the shadow of the rock as they ate, staring at Beatrice and occasionally at Lionel. The captain told Jenkins to avert his gaze, but he continued to stare at them throughout the day and on the ride that took them into the night.

They mounted up after eating and rode slowly back through the woods to which Lionel and Beatrice had become so accustomed. The captain let Lionel and Beatrice ride on Ulysses, but this ride was different from the previous ones.

Their grandfather rode most of the way back to the lodge with the captain. Riding side by side, they spoke, occasionally pointing out to each other various aspects of the nature of the landscape that surrounded them.

Lionel half expected that at any moment Beatrice would turn the horse and try to make another escape. But this never happened. Beatrice looked tired and rode for the rest of the day slumped forward, asleep against Lionel's back.

It started to rain sometime in the afternoon, and fell in cold, wet drops until they were all thoroughly soaked. Lionel shivered uncontrollably, but Beatrice woke up and pulled him closer, letting the rain pour over her head and back as she covered his.

They arrived in the meadow after dark, and Lionel thought that the little lodge looked sad as they rode past the smokehouse. The captain ordered his men to bivouac in the yard that led past the lodge to the garden, and within the half hour, their tents were set and their cook fires dotted the small valley's lawn.

The soldiers brought the children and their

grandfather to the lodge that had once been their home, and although they weren't tied, it was obvious that they were, once again, prisoners. Beatrice was half asleep, slumped against Lionel, and their grandfather had to carry her, ducking his head to get under the crooked door. Lionel watched as he cradled Beatrice in his arms and laid her on the buffalo robe in front of the crumbling fireplace.

Jenkins had wrecked the lodge. Their stores were overturned and what little furniture there was was broken. Lionel saw his reflection in a sliver of broken glass on the floor and thought that they couldn't have looked more different from their captors. Their hair had grown, and now even Lionel's could hold the feathers and strips of felt and leather wound tightly within. Lionel looked at the soldiers in their uniforms and then at his and Beatrice's buckskins. The buckskins blended into this world; the uniforms did not. Their grandfather stood at Lionel's side as the soldiers left, his attire somewhere in between.

Corn Poe was oddly quiet, as were Tom Gunn and eventually Barney Little Plume, who joined them but ended up standing quietly in the shadows of the lodge, avoiding where Beatrice lay. Beatrice was silent and expressionless, almost as if she wasn't there.

Brother Finn saw that the children were fed, and then at Grandpa's urging, they all bedded down in front of the crumbled fireplace for the night. No one argued, and soon they fell into a deep sleep accompanied by the crack and pop of the fire.

Beatrice's coughing woke Lionel in the middle of the night. It was heavier now, and sounded wet. Beatrice, wrapped in an army blanket and the buffalo robe, lay shivering at the edge of the fire's glow, covered with sweat. Lionel woke his grandfather, who told him that he would look after her and that he should go back to sleep. Lionel tried to stay awake, watching his grandfather wet Beatrice's head with cold water from the stream, but must have fallen asleep sometime during the night.

Lionel dreamed that night, and once again found himself on the shores of the great grass sea. He stood alone this time, holding the bear claws in his hand, looking out on the watery green. Great waves and whitecaps rose, and he could see Beatrice out in their turbulent midst. She was alone on her raft, the winds pushing her farther and farther from shore, farther and farther away from Lionel.

When Lionel awoke again it was still dark. His grandfather sat with Beatrice's head cradled in his lap. He sang a low song to her, but no longer pressed the cold compress against her forehead. Lionel looked at his grandfather and knew that Beatrice was gone.

He sat with his grandfather and Beatrice until morning. He felt numb and thought that it wasn't possible that Beatrice would leave. That Beatrice would leave him. But she had. Beatrice had told them that she wasn't going back to the reservation, and she was right.

CHAPTER THIRTY-FIVE

THE CAPTAIN'S WORDS • NINAIMSSKAAHKOYINNIMAAN, OR BEATRICE'S MEDICINE BUNDLE • A NEW PLACE IN THE WOOD

BY MORNING the freezing rain had turned to snow. Lionel's grandfather informed the captain of the events that had transpired overnight, and the captain appeared at the crooked door of the lodge looking genuinely distressed. He asked Corn Poe, Tom Gunn, and Barney to leave, and then stood in front of the crumbled chimney with his hat in hand and his head hung low.

"I'm not sure what to say," he offered to Lionel, but Lionel didn't hear him. He was lost. Lost without Beatrice. He stood at his grandfather's side with his sister wrapped in an army blanket at their feet.

At his grandfather's urging, Lionel had gathered Beatrice's few articles and laid them out on the floor next to her. There wasn't much—a few odd buttons of silver, gold, and mother-of-pearl, a couple of coins, some smooth rocks and pebbles from the stream, Corn Poe's pinecone, and the soft leather tobacco pouch that their grandfather had given her on her ninth birthday.

Lionel's grandfather asked the captain if they could borrow the great horse Ulysses and informed him that they would like to bury Beatrice in the traditional way of the Blackfeet, rather than leave her in the plot with the wooden markers at the edge of the outpost next to the boarding school. The captain agreed, and their grandfather went to attend to the horse, leaving Lionel standing in the cavernous room with his sister and the captain.

The captain shifted uncomfortably before breaking the morning's eerie silence. "Lionel, I'm sorry. Sorry for everything. I don't understand these times, and I'm sure it's worse for you."

Lionel looked up at the captain. He felt the numbness leave his face. A burning sensation filled his cheeks, soon to be replaced by uncontrollable tears. The captain knelt down and took him into his arms, letting Lionel's tears roll down the front of his uniform and the ribboned medals.

"I don't understand. After all that, how she could just die?" Lionel sobbed.

The captain pulled him closer. "She was sick, Lionel, and she has been for some time. I don't know that she ever fully recovered. I'm not sure how to explain it, but your sister—well, Beatrice's—her lungs—they were susceptible—" But the captain's tears stopped him.

It didn't make sense to Lionel either way. Despite the coughing, she had seemed fine to him. More than fine. She was his hero.

"Is that Beatrice's medicine bundle?" the captain asked, collecting himself by looking over the articles spread out on the floor.

Lionel glanced at Beatrice's meager belongings, choking back his tears. "Medicine bundle?"

"*Ninaimsskaahkoyinnimaan.*" The captain stared, lost, into the fireplace. "It's a collection of particular items that have a special meaning or power to you. Things you might want to keep with you in life . . . or to pass along in death."

The captain rummaged through the various skins and furs that lay scattered on the floor where the children slept.

"Here," the captain said, clearing his throat. "If you don't mind." He located a soft piece of doeskin and returned to where Lionel stood next to Beatrice.

"We'll check with your grandfather, but if you gathered her things, they could be placed in this skin and sewed shut. That would be Beatrice's medicine bundle. For someone to hold on to."

Lionel thought about it. These items were important to Beatrice. They meant something and somehow held some kind of power that she knew while she was still alive. Lionel thought about the bundle and then thought about what Brother Finn had told him about his soul. His soul was like a medicine bundle. It carried the experiences and adventures, good or bad, that he had throughout his life, the adventures and experiences that he had shared with Beatrice. Now, there was this remaining bundle, Beatrice's bundle. Was this an extension of Beatrice's life and experiences? Were these inanimate objects symbolic of the moments that made up some of the tiny pieces of Beatrice's soul?

Lionel gathered her items and placed them on

the doeskin. He added the bow and some of the arrows that they had made with their grandfather. His grandfather returned, and after speaking briefly with the captain, the captain left.

Lionel explained to his grandfather about the medicine bundle, and his grandfather told him that the captain was right. He said that the captain was a smart man.

Lionel's grandfather took the hawk's feather from Beatrice's hair and the Frozen Man's knife that she had liberated from Jenkins from her belt and laid them next to the rest of the items. Lionel took a blue jay feather and the eagle feather from his hair, but then paused, thinking about the bear claws. Beatrice might need them where she was going. She might see the Frozen Man and want to offer them back to him. He took the Frozen Man's bear claws from his neck and laid them with the feathers on top of Beatrice's buttons, coins, and stones. Lionel tucked the tobacco pouch and the Frozen Man's knife next to Corn Poe's pinecone, and sat back on his haunches. His grandfather nodded, and after repositioning the bow and arrows, folded the doeskin over, and with a long piece of rawhide string, stitched the opposing ends shut.

"You'll keep this, Lionel, you understand me?" his grandfather asked, handing him the bundle. "No matter where you go or what you do, you hold it for Beatrice. It's important for all of us."

Lionel took the bundle, and it was never too far from his side for the rest of his life.

Grandpa picked Beatrice up in his arms and carried her to the crooked doorframe. She looked small in his arms. Lionel followed, and as they stepped out of the lodge and into the meadow, he saw that Ulysses was standing in front of them with the travois from Grandpa's mule hitched to his harness, its poles leaning on Ulysses's strong haunches.

His grandfather placed Beatrice on the travois. He picked Lionel up and set him on the big horse's back. Grandpa swung up behind Lionel, and Ulysses stepped forward into the fresh and falling snow as if he knew exactly where he was going.

Lionel saw the government men in their uniforms all stop what they were doing and watch as their somber procession left the meadow and slowly made its way into the dark forest of the Great Wood. They rode for the better part of an hour to a place that, despite all of his rambling, Lionel did not recognize.

The trees were knotted and their branches bent into strange, almost fantastic configurations, often doubling back on themselves in swirling, living tangles.

As they traveled farther into this forest within a forest Lionel saw feathers and small pieces of colored material hanging from various branches and secured around the bending trees' trunks. He also saw that there were bones dangling from strips of rawhide, and skulls resting in the cruxes of the trees' upper branches. They continued, and Lionel saw horses ahead of them tied off in a small stand of trees that stood dwarfed by their giant counterparts.

As they approached the horses, Lionel saw Corn Poe up in one of the trees, securing what looked like a small raft or a bed. Brother Finn, Tom Gunn, and Barney stood on the ground below him, handing him strips of rawhide and rope to keep the tiny bed in place. Corn Poe jumped down from the tree when they approached.

"Hey, Lionel" was all he said, and then he stepped aside, next to Brother Finn, Barney, and Tom Gunn, who stood with their chins to their chests.

Lionel's grandfather sang softly as he dismounted, lifted Beatrice from the travois, and carried her toward the bed in the tree. Lionel followed and watched as he raised her up into the branches and set Beatrice in her resting place. Tears welled in his eyes, but he thought about Beatrice's strength and fought the tears back as best he could. He wasn't successful.

They stood in the woods listening to Grandpa's singing and the wind that rushed through the treetops. Birds sang, and there were long shafts of light illuminating slivered sections of the forest floor. After some time, Grandpa put his hand on Lionel's shoulder and turned back toward the horses. Corn Poe, Tom Gunn, Barney, and Brother Finn followed, leaving Lionel standing in the bent shadows of the small stand of trees.

Lionel knew it was time to go and that he would never see his sister in this form again, so he climbed the tree to be next to her one last time. The bending tree that held her wasn't high, and as if he had just climbed a ladder, he soon sat on the branch at her side.

Beatrice looked beautiful and in the buckskins that their grandfather had made her, every bit the black-masked warrior that Lionel would always remember. He could still see her high up on Ulysses's back, riding across the plains and into the mountains.

Lionel took her cold hand in his and studied her face. Beatrice looked at ease, almost peaceful where she lay, looking up through the canopy of the Great Wood toward the endless skies that waited overhead. Lionel held her hand in his for a moment longer, and then dropped from the tree and joined his grandfather, Corn Poe, Tom Gunn, Barney, and Brother Finn, who stood by the horses, waiting with a steady trail of tears falling from their eyes.

CHAPTER THIRTY-SIX

LEAVING THE MEADOW • JENKINS AND LUMPKIN • GOOD-BYE TO TOM GUNN AND BARNEY LITTLE PLUME • BACK TO THE BOARDING SCHOOL • INACCURATE WHISPERS • BEATRICE MOVES ON

LIONEL COULD never remember much of the days that followed. They returned to the meadow and gathered their belongings for the journey back to the boarding school. Unlike before, Lionel was anxious to leave the lodge. Without Beatrice, the fallen cabin wasn't the same. Corn Poe was quiet but stayed close to Lionel's side, offering to help him in any way he could.

Lionel looked around and remembered that when they had arrived, the meadow had been covered with snow. Now, in early autumn, the snows came but melted away with the morning sun. Lionel wondered if someday his people, like the snow, like Beatrice, would also melt away, but then thought that no matter how many times he had seen the snows come and go, they always returned.

Lionel and Corn Poe rode out of the meadow bareback on Ulysses, the great horse sandwiched between the captain and the rest of the soldiers who had made up the search party. Lionel's grandfather rode on his mule next to the captain and Brother Finn, but very little was said during the three days that it took them to ride back to the boarding school.

They rode east, parallel to the stream on what Lionel realized must have been the southern border of the Great Wood. Lionel noticed that with every step of the horses, the terrain that surrounded them changed. The vastness of the woods soon gave way to rounded foothills with clumps of trees, mostly pine, aspen, and birch; and these foothills soon opened into the endless sea of grass that Lionel and Beatrice had crossed at the start of their journey in the early spring of this year.

When they cleared the last of the wooded hills, they stopped to water the horses, and Lionel stood with the forest to his back, looking out across the plain, half expecting to see Beatrice in her tiny raft navigating the great swell of grass that rose and fell before him.

Sometime during their first night in the vast openness of the plains, Jenkins and Lumpkin escaped, choosing lives on the run rather than face what awaited them when they returned to the outpost. Lionel hoped that he never had to see them again.

The day before they reached the school, Tom Gunn and Barney were taken by a detachment of soldiers back down to their school at Heart Butte. Tom Gunn apologized to Lionel, and gave him his pocketknife before they left. Barney tried to apologize but broke down sobbing instead.

They rode on, and soon the rolling grass hills began to look familiar and Lionel felt as though he was revisiting a distant dream. Word arrived at the boarding school before their return, and as they rode into the dusty streets of the outpost, people came out of their shops and businesses to stand and stare as the renegade horsemen slowly passed.

The children of the school were gathered around the cluster of military buildings when the small party arrived. They pushed and pulled at each other trying to get a glimpse of the new boy, Corn Poe, and they reached out to touch Lionel in his buckskins and braided hair as the two boys rode, still on the captain's horse, past the barracks and the officers' quarters up to Ulysses's corral.

The school children spoke in hushed whispers about Beatrice and the men who had killed her, but as the horses passed over the last of the fading green grass of summer, it began to snow, and Lionel knew that no matter what the people said, no matter how the story was told, a simple bullet from a government gun could never kill Beatrice. Beatrice was somewhere and she would live forever.

EPILOGUE

IN THE END it was decided that Lionel, along now with Corn Poe, should return to school. They were turned over to the boarding school's administrators who immediately stripped them of their buckskins, issued them uniforms, and took them to the outpost's barber.

Lionel and Corn Poe sat on rough pine benches in a cold concrete room while their hair was cut away in chunks and scattered on the floor around them. Lionel looked over at Corn Poe and the relatively pale skin of his exposed scalp and couldn't help, for the first time in days, but smile.

In no time, he and Corn Poe were laughing.

They laughed, despite reprimand, both thinking about the lodge in the meadow and their long summer days spent running through the Great Wood. They thought about Mr. Hawkins and Junebug and the sweat lodge with Barney and Tom Gunn from Heart Butte. They thought about the wolverine and the bear and the stories of Napi the Old Man, and they laughed about the infuriated look that Beatrice had been able to instill on Jenkins's and Lumpkin's scowling faces. This was a laughter that was, as is the case with young boys, beyond control. For this was a laughter that could not, no matter what the governments, teachers, or Jenkinses of the world said or did, be silenced.

The adjustment back to school was difficult for Lionel and Corn Poe, but they both worked hard and eventually finished their yearly studies. Lionel's grandfather moved down into town for the winter to be closer and took a small room in the back of a lumber mill, where he swept the floors and watched over the place at night.

In the spring, Lionel's grandfather took what little money he had saved, and with the two boys as his partners, invested in a small herd of cattle. The herd was matched cow for cow by the government, and when the snows melted, they moved their outfit to graze on their own "reservation," the small plot on the banks of the Milk River near the northern end of the Blackfeet's allotted lands.

Glossary

Common Blackfoot Terms and Expressions

O'káát!: Sleep!

Nítssksinii'pa: I know.

Ássa! Póóhsapoot: Hey! Come here!

Saaám: medicine or powers of healing

Sstsiiysskaan: sweat lodge

Kitáí'kó'pohpa?: Are you afraid?

Niitsítapi: (literally) "real people"; original people

Po-no-kah-mita: "elk-dog" or horse

Nioomítaa: a great horse

Ninaimsskaahkoyinnimaan: medicine bundle

OTHER TERMS

Travois: a vehicle used by Plains Indians to carry loads over rough terrain. It consisted of two trailing poles that formed a frame for a load-bearing platform or netting. It could be harnessed to a horse or pulled by hand or a shoulder harness.

Counting Coo: To count "coo" or "coup" means to touch an armed enemy with a special stick called a coup stick, or with the hand. The touch is not a blow, but serves to indicate how close a warrior could get to his enemy and escape unharmed. As an act of bravery, counting coup was regarded as greater than killing an enemy in single combat, greater than taking a scalp or horses or any prize.

Fourth of July Pow-Wow: A Pow-Wow is Native American Indian ceremony or organized social get-together. At the time of this story, the U.S. government only allowed these to take place as a celebration of the signing of the Declaration of Independence on July 4. Independence Day was the only time that tribes were allowed to engage in traditional practices.

References

Coombes, Allen J. *Trees*. London: Dorling Kindersley Handbooks, 1992.

Duvall, D.C., and Wissler, Clark. *Mythology of the Blackfoot Indians*. Lincoln: University of Nebraska Press, 1995.

Farr, William E. *The Reservation Blackfeet, 1882–1945: A Photographic History of Cultural Survival*. Seattle: University of Washington Press, 1984.

Frantz, Donald G. *Blackfoot Grammar*. Toronto: University of Toronto Press, 1991.

Frantz, Donald G., and Russell, Norma Jean. *Blackfoot Dictionary*. 2nd ed. Toronto: University of Toronto Press, 1995.

Grinnell, George Bird. *Blackfoot Lodge Tales: The*

Story of a Prairie People. Lincoln: Bison Books, 1962.

Harrod, Howard L. *The Animals Came Dancing: Native American Sacred Ecology and Animal Kinship*. Tuscon: University of Arizona Press, 2000.

———. *Mission Among the Blackfeet*. Norman: University of Oklahoma Press, 1971.

Linderman, Frank Bird (1869–1938). "Indian Why Stories." Edited by Simon Plouffe. Champaign: Project Gutenberg, 1996. <http://infomotions.com/etexts/gutenberg/dirs/etext96/inwhy10.htm>

Macfarlan, Allan A., and Casey, Kathy, ed. *Native American Tales and Legends*. Mineola, N.Y.: Dover Publications, 1968.

ACKNOWLEDGMENTS

Many thanks to my editor, Jennifer Besser, without whom this novel would not have been written; and to Beth Clark, Monica Mayper, and everyone at Disney-Hyperion.

Thanks also to my friends and family who patiently read the many unpolished drafts and offered their opinions, support, and advice.

And a special thanks to the Blackfeet Nation, whose history and enduring culture continue to inspire.

QUESTIONS

for James Crowley, author of *Starfish*

1) When did you first become interested in the history of Native Americans?

I'm not sure, as I've been interested in Native American culture for as long as I can remember. I spent a lot of time outdoors as a kid, so I was always fascinated by the close connection that Native American cultures have with the natural world. I was drawn to their traditions and mythology, which reflect the Native Americans' heightened awareness of their surroundings. I remember one time walking through a forest. The trees were immense and took my breath away. But what was amazing to me is that everyone I was with suddenly started to whisper as if we had walked into a great cathedral, mosque, or synagogue. And, in effect we had. It was amazing. There were no signs asking people to keep their voices down; it just happened. A natural reaction. It seems that Native American cultures were more in tune with that. In tune with what made us whisper, and I think it's worth paying attention to.

2) What inspired you to tell a story about this particular time period?

I loved reading comic books as a kid (still do), which rely heavily on pictures to tell the story. I see stories that way. First the images come to mind, and then I try to convey those images through words. With *Starfish*, my inspiration started with the image of Beatrice and Lionel, although then they didn't have names at the time. I could just see two kids on a horse running or returning back to nature.

I knew the story would be set around 1900, but didn't have the exact year in mind until I sat down and started the research. And then I became fascinated with 1909 as a kind of transition year. The big push west for European immigrant exploration was winding down, but the inevitable settlement that followed was now becoming evident. I kept coming back to the idea that many people alive in 1909 would have seen firsthand the change from the Great Plains societies to the largely European settlement of the West. And the world was about to become a much smaller place with World War I just around the corner. It was also a time just before a large part of the Blackfeet lands would become Glacier National Park. For me, this transition time or "crossroads" in many ways echoes Lionel and Beatrice's journey.

3) What research did you do to help you write a historically accurate story about the internment of the Blackfeet?

A few years ago, my work in film brought me to a job on the Blackfeet Reservation in Browning, Montana. I had heard about the existence of boarding schools (the inspiration for the Chalk Bluff boarding school), but I knew very little about their history. While spending time in Blackfeet country, I worked with several people who had either attended boarding schools like these or had relatives who had. Hearing their stories inspired me to do further research. I started with visits to the Museum of the Plains Indian and contacted the Piegan Institute in Browning. Their bookstores and recommended reading lists from their Web sites were highly influential as well. One book in particular, *The Reservation Blackfeet, 1882–1945: A Photographic History of Cultural Survival*, edited by Dr. William E. Farr, was a great resource for me—the book is full of so many intriguing and haunting images that were really hugely impactful. And then, of course, one text would answer questions while simultaneously causing me to ask others, leading me to the next book.

4) There is a scene in the book in which some of the characters breach Blackfeet tradition. Why did you add this into the story?

In the sweat lodge scene, I wanted to show how Beatrice, Lionel, and the Heart Butte boys have a desire to connect with Blackfeet customs, even if the results are imprudent. Being raised at the boarding schools meant they were forbidden from speaking their own language and participating in any kind of Blackfeet religious ceremony, and so they must interpret the traditions on their own—which leads to some big missteps, like Beatrice taking part in the sweat lodge ceremony. They very innocently get things wrong. This scene was important to me because I also wanted to demonstrate the danger of true customs being lost in the face of the U.S. government's assimilation policies. Beatrice in particular fights to hold on to Blackfeet customs, despite being told not to at school. In part, this defiance stems from her strong-willed character; on a deeper level, it's a way for her to connect with her ancestry, to something larger than herself (even if that means figuring it out on her own). But she's also a child who lost her parents at a very young age, and so a connection to the traditions of her ancestry means a connection to her parents, to her family.

5) Why did choose the title *Starfish*?

Choosing a title is tough. You write a story that is more than three hundred pages long and then try to sum it all up in a word or two. For me, the starfish is an important symbol in the book for a couple of reasons. One is that it ties in to the water theme that runs throughout the story. On my first visit to the Blackfeet Reservation and to Montana, I was struck by how the rise and fall of the hills on the plains that lead to the Rocky Mountains look like rolling waves of water. Water also has great spiritual meaning in Blackfeet culture. As Grandpa mentions in the novel, the Blackfeet avoid fishing because of their belief that the Suyitapis, or Underwater People, inhabit rivers and lakes. The Suyitapis are a source of power for sacred items, such as medicine bundles. Then there's the moment when Mr. Hawkins shows Lionel a starfish. It's a childhood memento, from a faraway place, which I hoped would demonstrate Mr. Hawkins's own journey. It also initiates a conversation between Lionel and Mr. Hawkins that explores the larger themes in the book—ideas about assimilation, as well as about resilience and adaptability. Lionel is experiencing firsthand the U.S. government's assimilation policies and their attempts to eradicate Native American culture. He knows that, like the starfish, people have been displaced from their environment, with devastating results. But Mr. Hawkins also discusses the idea of resilience, something he sees in Lionel and his sister. To me, Lionel and Beatrice are two incredibly resilient characters. They survive even the harshest conditions on their journey—being lost, freezing cold, and nearly starving. We see Lionel's struggle to adapt—to reconcile the stories Grandpa tells with those he's learned at school, especially in the face of a great loss. And hopefully we see Beatrice's perseverance in safeguarding Blackfeet customs, traditions, stories, and spiritual beliefs in her life and that of her brother.

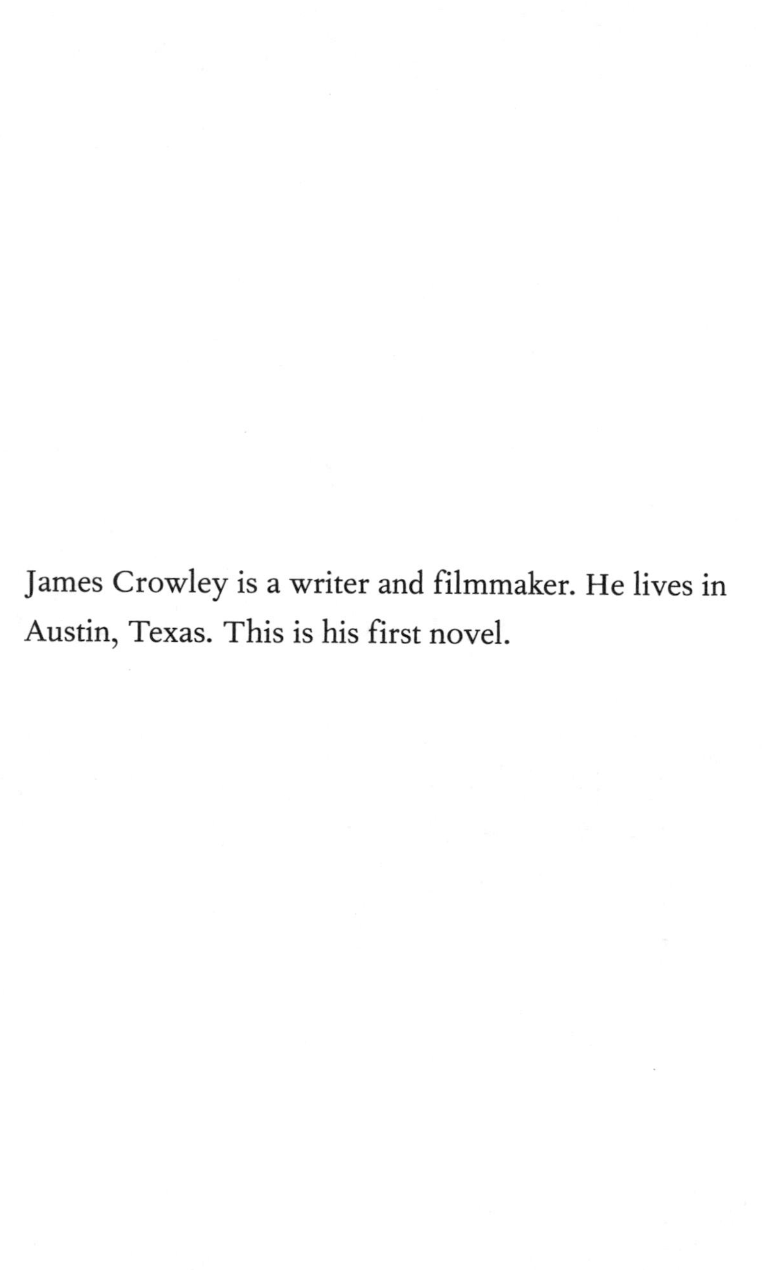

James Crowley is a writer and filmmaker. He lives in Austin, Texas. This is his first novel.